Praise for the Base Branch Series

"Megan Mitcham's books are well-paced, well-plotted suspense novels edged with stunning sensual intensity. Her lovers are cold and deadly--except when they are skin-to-skin. I can't wait for the next book in the series!"

- **DELILAH DEVLIN**
New York Times and USA Today bestselling author

"Nail-biter all the way to the end."

- **Michelle**, MsRomanticReads
Adult Romance & Erotic Book Reviews

"This is a fresh and exciting story with lots of great characters."

- **5 Star Amazon Review**, Enemy Mine

"Megan now joins my elite team of must read authors. I fell in love with her work in *Enemy Mine*, and it just gets better the more I read."

- **TNT Reviews**

BOOKS BY MEGAN MITCHAM

BASE BRANCH NOVELS
ENEMY MINE
JUSTICE MINE
STRANGER MINE
WARRIOR MINE
DANGER MINE
PRISONER MINE
VERSIONS
VIRTUES
VARIATIONS
SURVIVOR MINE - 2017

BUREAU NOVELS
FOR ALL TO SEE
PAINTED WALLS
FORD'S BOOK - 2017

ANTHOLOGIES
ANTICIPATION
CONQUESTS
ROGUES
SEX OBJECTS
COWBOY HEAT
HIGH OCTANE HEROES
WILD AT HEART VOLUME II
benefiting Turpentine Creek Wildlife Refuge

Versions

Base Branch Novella #7

Megan Mitcham

Copyright Warning

Published by MM Publishing LLC

Edited by Lacey Thacker

Proofread by Tina Rucci & Lynn Mullan

Cover Design by Deranged Doctor Designs

Versions
All Rights Are Reserved. Copyright 2016 by Megan Mitcham

Versions

Second electronic publication: August 2016
Second print publication: August 2016

Digital ISBN: 978-1-941899-08-3

Print ISBN: 978-1-941899-09-0

To the trials of life, for every heartache, scrape, slight, and failure reveals true character. May our mettle be bright and enduring, and bring us closer to the people we are meant to become.

Chapter One

"Rin! Sorry I'm late, babe," Nate hollered through the condo loudly enough for every occupant in the three-story building to hear.

The thunderous boom broke the serenity of her MAC makeover experience. She jerked at the abrupt noise she'd expected a half an hour before. The ultra-red lipstick she was applying jumped over the light-pink edge of her upper lip, making a mockery of her hard work.

"Damn."

Rin sifted through bottles of cleanser, several different shades of eyeliner, palettes of shadow, and powders until she found the pack of specialty wipes. Plucking one from the container, she leaned closer to the vanity mirror and sought the best angle of attack before neatly wiping it away. Nate's hefty steps drew near. She whirled in a hurry to catch his reaction to the "new" Darinda Lee.

"Traffic was a bitch named Suzy."

She smiled at his crazy saying, while her body hummed at his deep timbre and the knowledge of what was about to go down. Because, late or not, sick or not, when Nate came home he came home inside her...or on her.

"Well, I'm not a jealous girlfriend, but next time tell Suzy I get psycho when anything gets between me and my man."

"I'll be sure and let her know."

He stopped so quickly rounding the corner his sneakers *squeaked* on the wood of their bedroom floor. His fist tightened around the straps of his gym bag, highlighting the bulging veins coursing down his arm. The dark brown of his eyes turned cold, something that had scared her when they'd first met. But now the obsidian glaze incited the driving pulse in her damp panties. He tossed the bag to the floor. Its *thud* echoed in the minimalist space.

"Who are you and what have you done with Rin?"

"You didn't really want her. What a snooze fest in bad clothes. Can you honestly tell me her boxy accountant's suits and dull hair got you hot?"

Nate stalked forward. His bulky lineman's frame filled the arched doorway leading to the massive—by DC standards—walk-in closet and double vanity. He raked a hand over the snake-print leather covering her hip. His hand dipped at her narrow waist and rose higher. Heat plumped her breast through the sleeveless sheath dress. A moan parted her lips.

"Her clothes? No. Her reactions? Yes. Her body? Yes." Nate gripped her chin and angled it down ever so slightly, since in heels she stood nearly an inch taller than he. "Rin would have known not to bother with lipstick until I've had my fill." His thumb smeared over her lower lip. "Babe." He flipped a lock of bright blonde hair—four or five shades lighter than her former color—between his thumb and forefinger. "She would have known I don't care how her hair looks, as long as it's tangled in my hands while I'm fucking her."

"Yes," she pleaded. Her hips danced in tiny circles, rubbing her clit across the span of his prospering erection.

"Tell me why, Rin. Why change your look? We've been together six months. Doesn't the taste of my cum on your tongue nearly every damn day tell you I'm satisfied?"

"Mmm, it does." She licked her lip and caught the tip of his thumb. Salt seared her taste buds. Nate's nostrils flared and Rin pressed her aching nipples against his impossibly hard pecs. "But...I'm only seven months out of a master's program and I looked like the ladies who've worked at the DOD since the Reagan administration. I've been there long enough that I have a reputation based on my merits, not the length of my legs—"

"Which fit perfectly around my barrel waist." Nate nestled his cock in the junction of her thighs, his fingers bit into her ass, and he held them together.

"Ahhh, they do. And now I can wear fitted things without worrying they'll only see my body and not my mind."

"Don't wear this to the office. Defense would ship you to another country to entice them into signing a hundred-year treaty."

"I'd never wear this to work. I picked out some fancy suits from Moi-Même. But I'll wear this to dinner tonight with the gang."

"Man. I'd rather you wore it while wearing me out all night."

"If you'd quit talking and get moving, we'd have time for a quickie." She wrapped her arms around his neck and pulled him close, whispering against his mouth, "Or are you scared of a little lipstick?"

"I'm scared of a lot of things concerning you, but lipstick isn't one of them."   Her brow crinkled, something the consultants at the cosmetics counter would likely frown upon, without actually frowning. *What things scared him?* Their relationship had been live-in from nearly day one, but not so serious that he should have anxiety over it. Unless he wanted out. Or in deeper.

They'd never used the L word. She'd only said it to three people in her life and two of them were dead. The third wasn't long for the world.

She inhaled to ask, but his lips sealed over hers in a crushing embrace. It broke her unpleasant train of thought—a major one of the several reasons she liked having him around. Rin plowed her fingers through his close-cropped hair and parried his plundering tongue. Nate eased back, his thin and now-vibrant red lips spread into a grin.

"Not worried I'll get you dirty?"

"As a football coach's main squeeze," she glanced down at his hands still gripping her ass, "I've gotten used to the sweat. I like your smell." She dipped her head and licked the column of his neck. "And I like it when you get me dirty."

"You drive me crazy, Rin." He shoved her back and turned her to face the mirror. "Bend over and grab the sink."

Raw masculinity paraded itself in Nate's massive girth. It stood out on either side of her twig-like frame. His wet shirt clung to the curving dips and elevations of his full muscles. If ever a bulldog had been turned into a human, Nathaniel Harmon was the end result of that magic. His rough hike of her skirt jarred her hips. And, like always, she was thankful he respected her enough to leave her partially dressed while they got down and dirty. Her scars were too ugly for sex, probably for her more so than him.

Rin braced both hands on the cool metal of the faucet and looked to the mirror. In the reflection her gaze flashed to her lively hair color, which would take some getting used to, and then skittered to her heavy lidded baby-blues before jumping to Nate's devilish expression.

"Black lace. Nice. But I prefer your sleek, pink bare skin." One finger slid across her chilled bottom. It ran the ridge of her thong from the base of her tailbone to her sensitive whorl. A shock of desire clenched her sex. "Such a greedy little ass you have. It's a wonder your pussy gets any attention at all."

"You make me greedy, Nate. You make me so hot and needy." She pressed against his finger, but he removed it.

"Don't rush me, babe. Can't have you coming before I even get inside you."

"Why not?" she moaned.

"Because we'll save multiples for later. Right now, it's one big cumfest. You and me, together."

Rin bent her elbows and rubbed her engorged nipples on the edge of the counter, beyond desperate for release. The way Nate talked to her ramped her lust to a far off universe. At first it had shocked her speechless and she hadn't known why. In her wayward youth, which wasn't all that long ago, she'd done plenty worse things than let a guy whisper, "pussy," in her ear.

Lace glided over her cheeks, tickled her thighs, and landed atop the red Jimmy Choos she really should have saved for a separate shopping spree. But her promotion paid nearly double the salary and, from the taut jaw and laser stare at the curve of her backside, her boyfriend obviously adored them.

"You're dripping already. I don't even have to lap your clit."

Then again, maybe it wasn't the shoes he liked so much.

Nate dropped out of sight. His hot breath curled across her cunt. "But it doesn't mean I don't want to." The wet barb of his tongue scored her swollen nub. Once. Twice. Ten strokes in rapid succession.

"Ahhh, stop, baby, or I'm going to come," she panted, grinding her breasts against the white granite.

"Don't come."

Those two words were the only pause in attack on the little bundle of nerves. To dull the overwhelming urge to fly into a million pieces, Rin opened the top drawer and pulled out a gold foil package. As much sex as they had, they always practiced safe sex. She would have caved too many times, but Nate stuck to the agreement like the dirtiest saint in Catholicism.

She held it between her legs. "Please, Nate."

He pierced her with his naked tongue once more and then stood. His lips glistened in the bright lighting. His cheeks flushed. He licked her cream from his mouth. "You taste like a whore in heat, babe."

"I am, for you."

Nate stripped his athletic shorts, snagged the packet from her hand, and set about sheathing himself. Rin lowered her hand and panted into the sink. The long ends of her hair pooled in the dry basin. Insane. She must be insane. This relationship was nothing but sex between

roommates who happened to share mutual friends.
But hey, what relationship was perfect?

Alone worked for her. Lovey dovey did not.
Nate refused to leave her alone, even with her
upfront rules. He probably stuck around because of
them. What guy wouldn't want strings-free pussy
and a place to live?

His blunt head swirled in the juices at her
entrance. Suddenly, she no longer cared about
anything but penetration and the ride. She arched
and pressed back. Nate's meaty hands gripped her
hips, churning her tumult higher.

"Let's see if this cunt is as tight as I
remember."

"You were in it this morning."

"And it's been too long."

"Yes. Yes." She writhed.

He stretched her so full. Her breath caught as
it always did. Nate grunted, pushing to the base.
They weren't the best fit. He never hit her G spot,
but what he lacked in length he more than made
up for in girth and finesse. He set a punishing pace,
his body lurching as he jacked himself inside her,
enlivening her slick folds with each forceful smack
of their flesh.

"Tight as ever," he chuffed.

"Tight enough to make you a minute man?"

"Oh, Rin." Nate grimaced and his fingers
loosened on her hip. He leaned forward and
presented his thumb. "Lick it." Having an idea of
where that digit was headed, she left enough saliva
on his pad to do the job. "That's it, babe."

When the slippery pressure of Nate's thumb
whirled over her pulsing rosette her mouth fell
open. The sorcery of his fast beat combined with
the heavy tension at the base of her spine. Rin
spiraled out of control. She pressed her nipples

against the counter and moaned. "I can't stop. I'm coming. Oh, Nate it feels so good."

"Fuck," he roared. Before her eyes closed on blinding ecstasy, the veins in Nate's wide neck bulged and his chin arched toward the ceiling. He pushed her through the exquisite spasm of every overwrought nerve ending in her body. She came violently, pulsing around his shaft, which fought back with thrusts and swelling throbs of shooting cum.

Rin rested her cheek on the cold countertop and worked to rein in her composure. She loved the high of foreplay and the exploit of two bodies consuming one another, but she hated the vulnerability of the drop. That time when the carnal act became something more than pleasure. When sex became emotion. Where emotion became commitment, which ultimately turned to disillusionment.

Nate crowded her with his big chest. He brushed her long hair to the side with gentle strokes. The warmth of his lips brushed over her shoulder in a ghost of a kiss before he straightened.

"We have to meet Zach and Jen at eight," she panted.

"That gives us forty-five to get there. I'll be out of the shower in seven."

"On the dot?" she asked with a giggle.

"Give or take a few, smart ass." His palm stung her cheek in a playful smack.   That opened her eyes right up. She shifted to her elbows and watched Nate disengage from her body. He slipped the condom off his waning erection, tossed it in the garbage under the sink, and stripped off his shirt. Of course he left his damn clothes in the middle of the walkway.

"You know, the hamper is four feet from your heap of sweaty clothes just inside the open closet door?"

"In perfect shooting distance for you, babe. Just remember, it's all in the wrist."

"You know, you're a jerk?"

"Yep. The only question is, why do you put up with it?"

She shook her head and eyed his sturdy ass as it disappeared into the bathroom. When the shower squeaked on she turned back to her reflection. It would take a while to get used to the new 'do and makeup, but she liked it a lot. Now, if she could just get the rest of herself unrumpled.

Snagging a washcloth, Rin wet it and cleaned between her legs. It took a wiggle or five to get the leather over her bottom and smoothed back into place. Then she grabbed Nate's clothes and threw them, along with the rag, into the dirty clothes basket. Whistling reverberated from the glass-walled shower stall.

Was that the Sesame Street theme song?

"You're killing me," she hollered while crossing the two steps to the steam-filled room and then closing the door. "Sing or yodel. Do anything but whistle."

Seriously, how had she managed to maintain her sanity over the last several months? She snatched the brush from the vanity with a little more force than necessary and dragged the bristles through her straight-as-a-line boob-length hair. At least screwing hadn't messed with the bit of volume she'd teased at the roots. Rin leaned forward and smoothed a hand over the angular structure of her face.

A vibration tickled her hand. She jerked, the brush clutched like a hammer, ready to drop on an unassuming bug. Nate's sleek black phone settled. Rin released a long exhale and set the brush down. *Way to freak out over a text, Lee.*

She set the brush down and reached for the phone, thinking it might be Zach or Gregory changing plans as they often did on a whim. Her hand froze over the lit screen. That long exhale turned into a vacuum in her lungs. All function seized, except sight.

Rin read the text. Paused. And then read it again. And again.

The more she read the less sense it made.

The CAL urn came back negative for human remains. It was tree ash. Quit playing house and stay focused. She may make contact.

Chapter Two

Human remains? Nate coached a championship football team. He taught kids on a roller-coaster-cocktail of pubescent hormones how to handle a car without killing themselves. Occasionally—and even more dicey than dodging head-on collisions—he talked reproductive systems while subbing in health class. Not even college-level health classes discussed cremated bodies.

Playing house? With who? Her? Someone else?

No. No, to all of it. Rin pulled in a shaky breath. This was obviously a wrong number. The lingo sounded cop-ish. They lived in the capital, where the crime rate kept pace with the ever-expanding population. Surely a cop's fat fingers dialed the wrong number.

Weird. Just weird.

A shiver wracked Rin's body. She chaffed her arms to ward off the chill, but couldn't. She stumbled back from the phone and into the closet. She clutched the stand of shelves to the right of the door, steadied her wobbling legs, and perused half her wardrobe without actually seeing it.

The shower cut off. She almost jumped out of her heels. He hadn't been in there long at all... because they were going to have dinner with their friends and they were running late...because they'd just fucked like feral beasts. Rin's pulse lurched despite her mental pep talk.

The bathroom door creaked and Nate's footsteps padded out, all high-pitched traces of the trilling annoyance gone. Rin didn't dare turn around. He'd call her a crazy fool for getting worked up over a text that had nothing to do with him plowing another woman. Then he'd laugh all night, sharing the story with their friends at her expense.

She was curious to see his reaction to the text though.

He passed behind her in the suddenly too-small closet. She swallowed an impossible knot.

"It's five-hundred degrees outside. Why are you looking for a jacket, babe?"

She cleared her throat. "Restaurants are always cold." Where had that come from? In a confrontation she usually stammered like an idiot and thought of the perfect retort the next day.

He shifted through some clothes and then tossed his towel into the hamper. His stubbly chin grazed her shoulder. "That's why you bring me along, to keep you warm." The deep rasp of his voice usually drove her to the corner of hot and horny, but now the nearness coagulated her blood.

She watched from her periphery as Nate left the closet with a pair of slacks and a button down slung over his bare shoulder, his phone in hand and his thumbs flying over the keys.

She waited for him to laugh. To tell her about the wacko who sent him a crazy message and the bullshit he'd put him through with his series of replies. She waited while he dressed, while he corralled her into a Jaguar coupe he shouldn't have been able to afford, while he weaved them in and out of traffic. But it never came.

The fancy car slid into an elusive end slot on the storefront's block on 14th. He shut off the engine and kicked his head to the side. "Babe, you're quiet as a corpse over there."

"Am I?" she replied. His phrase sank into her overburdened brain and she squinted to keep from going bug-eyed. "Guess you just screwed the sense out of me."

A smirk settled on his lips. "We're here. So, get your mind out of the gutter." When he got out and closed the door his chuckle dissipated. He sauntered around the front, his husky frame eating the space between the two cars like a midnight snack. Her door opened under his hand.

Rin forced a smile, planted her feet on the asphalt, stood, and sidled out of the way. But he shut the door and reeled her in close, banding his arms around her shoulders. Automatically, her arms encircled his middle as far as they could reach. Nate tugged her closer still, smothering her with a kiss.

Her fingers bumped hard metal at the small of his back—if anything about his bulkily muscled back could be considered small. The rigidity in her stance doubled. In the early days of their relationship, he'd packed a pistol everywhere they went. With staunch Republican views, Rin embraced his right to carry, but honestly she liked guns better in theory than reality. The longer they'd dated the less often he'd carried the thing—in deference to her, she'd thought.

"Why the pistol?"

"Because you've got me starched again." He ground his hardening length against her core.

"Very funny." Rin turned and tried to side-step out of his arms. She found herself barred, trapped between the car and his equally immovable chest. She should have liked it, would have liked it...before.

"I have it to keep you safe, babe."

Only she didn't feel safe at all. A pervading sense of isolation gnawed on her nape like a starved animal, as if the ground had opened up and swallowed everyone else in the world. Her swollen tongue wouldn't allow her to speak, but Nate didn't look to her to say anything. He snagged her hand and pulled. "Come on, hot stuff. Let's go have some fun."

She shuffled behind him on the neat sidewalk lined with buildings that were none too spectacular when considering the hype this street saw from droves of her peers. Nate hit his stride and her legs scissored in a quick flutter. The tight leather of her shoes rubbed the beginning of a blister onto her delicate skin. "Can you slow down a bit?"

"Yeah, sorry." He dropped back and wrapped her arm in the crook of his elbow. "Got a little overexcited I guess. It's been a hell of a day. I'm ready for a drink or ten."

"We should have taken a cab," she whispered.

"Nah. I want ten. I'll have one."

"Then maybe I'll have ten."

"That's my girl."

At the most swank eatery until Le Diplomate a few blocks up, they passed an outcropping of glass framed in thick rustic metal and then turned right. Through the concrete entrance the hostess's practiced hands ushered them across the stone floor to their waiting friends.

"Rin!" Jen squealed, hopping from her smooth wooden chair. "Get out. I freaking love your hair. And that dress. Oh my God, are those Choos?" The exuberant brunette fanned herself with Barcelona's extensive drink menu.

The crowd around them didn't skip a beat, caught in the din of their own merriment. This place did that and Rin was ready for some indulgence of her own.

"Perfect timing." Zach's green eyes shifted behind her, toward the kitchen.

Jen's breath caught and she leaned to the side, peering around the outfit she'd just gushed over. "Forget your Choos and get a load of our waiter. Please be our waiter. Please be our waiter."

"They're called servers," Gregory chimed with his charismatically crooked grin. He stood, leaned forward, and planted a big one square on Rin's lips. She released Nate and wrapped Gregory in a fierce hug. "And these days they tend to sue when ogled too forcibly. So, no groping." He winked and set her back next to Nate.

"Lawyers," Rin mirrored her best friend's lopsided grin. "Always spoil the fun."

She and Nate laughed for the first time since the text, but none of their friends noticed. They all stared in unabashed awe at the person coming to take their order.

"I'm ready to pick a team and erect my flag in the dirt. This guy seals the deal. Gay all the way. Sorry, ladies, but this nugget of manliness has finally made a decision." Gregory smoothed his hand over the cream cable-knit sweater that hid his leanly muscled physique.

"Erect your flag or your dick? In the ground or our server?" Jen asked. "I have zero qualms about calling him a server, because I'd let him service me any day."

"I prefer the latter." Gregory sat wide-eyed.

"Something's wrong with you two," Zach announced.

"But I don't see you looking away," Nate noted. "And I hope y'all know what you want to drink. Jen and Greg, your prayers are answered in three, two..."

Rin couldn't get over her friends' reaction to this guy enough to turn and look for herself. She needed this camaraderie to ease the sting of loneliness, even though Nate's beefy hand wrapped securely around her upper arm. The realization of the superficiality of their relationship—crazy text or not—raised the curtain and left her standing on stage in nothing but her sparkling personality.

"Evening, gentlemen. Ladies." The silken honey of the unfamiliar voice coated her nakedness in a soothing balm. The waiter cleared his throat. The low rumble vibrated very near her ear. "What can I get you, miss?"

She canted her head in his direction. Surprise smacked her square in the face. Smoldering bedroom eyes gazed into hers. The crystal blue orbs pierced through a strong brow and straight into her soul.

It was him.

Rin stepped back, stumbling over Nate's feet. A thud sounded her landing against her boyfriend's hard chest. Her heart competed with the sound, slamming into her ribs like it meant to escape.

"Whoa, there," the waiter said, maintaining an invisible grip on Rin that made it impossible to look away.

She didn't know him, but she'd been looking for him everywhere ever since that day. They'd shared nothing. Not to anyone else. Not a fuck. Not even a kiss. But she'd felt the momentary connection deeper than anything before... or after.

Blond hair only a shade darker than her own sat in disarray across his forehead, but was shorn close around his ears. The hint of a beard hugged the strongest jaw she'd ever seen. Lips the perfect shape and fullness made for hours and hours of kissing would have softened the blow his appearance delivered, if he'd only smile.

"You startled me," she said by way of explanation for her odd behavior.

No one knew about that day. There hadn't been anything to say.

Hey guys, I was waiting for the bus to my grandparents' house—by way of a rich suburb because I didn't want them to know where I came from—outside the Pentagon when a car rolled by bumping Marl Marly's Symphony. Only the first few whistled beats poured out the windows, but it had every ultra-whitey in line sneering at the overbearing base. My roots showed. Everyone except me and this guy with broad shoulders and unkept blond hair. His head bobbed to the music, while his eyes followed the car. The corners of his lips turned up and his hips rolled so hypnotically I forgot to step onto the transport.

People brushed past me and I didn't notice. I was too wrapped up in this guy's reaction. It was so like mine. So unlike everyone else's. His head pivoted. Our eyes locked for the longest, most intense eight count in my life. The encyclopedia of our lives passed between us in that one look. I knew meeting him would change my life forever, that love at first sight was real, to say nothing of love period— to which I'd been a life-long skeptic until that mind altering moment. Then he turned on his heels and walked away.

"Wasn't my intention." He said the words, but his head ticked to the side and his eyes flared in a way that opposed them.

"What's your name, gorgeous?" Jen asked.

"Call me Luck," the waiter said, holding Rin's befuddled gaze.

Nate steadied her and shifted to place himself between her and the...her and Luck, but a massive party of suits poured in to their left. They crowded the walkway with banter and briefcases. The man screwing with her head—more than her shrink ever had—could have stepped to the side of the table toward Zach. Instead, he stepped forward, crowding her with his sharply muscled chest tucked neatly into a waiter's white button down. Chiseled forearms and lightly sun-kissed skin exposed at his rolled sleeves.

Whether someone shoved him, or he took a dive she wasn't sure, but his sinewy chest suddenly plastered her front. One arm wrapped around her waist, catching her in a subtle dip. His other shot out to the chair back to steady them. She swore she heard Gregory moan. Luck's muscles in action did something sinful to her psyche.

"Jackass, I'm not into threesomes," Nate blustered just behind her head. She'd see him, if she'd tear her gaze off Luck. But she couldn't.

Luck lifted his heavy blue gaze from her for the first time and squared it on Nate. "Me neither."

Until that moment, she'd been sure Nate could have defended her honor or his ego against any man. He probably outweighed Luck by fifty muscle-dense pounds. Luck had a foot of height on him, but his calm voice and confident demeanor had her more than second guessing the outcome. Then again, Nate had a gun.

For the oddest reason, if the two got into it she didn't think that would matter.

"Luck," Rin said, drawing on the last stitch of her sanity, "how about you tip a girl upright and bring her a Peroni, a glass of Casarena cabernet, a

Goose Island, a Bourbon Spice Rack, and a Hot Delilah…make that two Delilah's." The first impression of a smile lightened the corner of his mouth. He straightened and released her, his hand sweeping firmly over the sway of her waist. The touch lingered for far too long. "Anyone else feeling a double?"

Whether they wanted it or not, her friends declined. Luck nodded and sauntered off as though he had not a care in the world. As though Nate didn't blow smoke from his ears behind her.

Rin pulled out the chair across from Gregory and sat.

"A double? Shit, I need a bottle *and* a cigarette after that." Jen gave her fan another workout.

"Shut up," Zach chided with a finger-shove to her shoulder, but he only spurred her giggles.

"Sit, babe." Rin pulled out Nate's chair and tugged his hand.

He sat with a huff. "That bastard better not show his face over here, if he knows what's good for him."

She rubbed her hands together and hoped she never saw him again. Luck. His name should have been Misfortune because he was the only person who'd ever looked at her and seen everything she struggled to hide every hour of every day.

Add him to the heap of crap she didn't understand about tonight.

"Here you are," another unfamiliar voice rumbled several minutes later.

In unison all the heads at their table snapped up, except hers. Rin already knew it wasn't *him*. Slowly she turned to a wide-smiling guy with chin-length brown hair. He deposited the drinks they'd ordered on the table in front of the person whose eyes lit up at the raising of their drink of choice. Good for the waiter that he got to Nate's last, because the surly sourpuss only glared at the tumbler of whiskey.

"I'm Pete and I'll be your server tonight. Can I get you guys started off with an appetizer or are you ready to hear our specials? Oh, by the way," he added with a shake of his finger, "the drinks have been taken care of."

Gregory and Jen's mouths gaped and they nearly clapped, while the other two only groaned.

"We'll need a few minutes, Pete. Thank you." Rin nodded.

"I'll check back with y'all in a few." He smiled and retreated to a table across the way.

Everything lulled for several beats. Rin looked off without seeing anything but the demons in her mind. Under the table, a shoe tapped her own, bringing her head around. Gregory's high cheeks flushed and his eyes widened in question. She gave an imperceptible shrug. She didn't know the question and she sure as hell didn't know the answer.

"You think the Skins will cover the spread on New Orleans this weekend?" Zach asked Nate, knowing well enough—from coaching together—to ease the tension.

"Only if Griffin's ankle can stand the action." Nate's response was half-hearted, but it only took two more questions about offense and turnovers before the men blazed down the He-Man-football path.

Jen sidled close to Gregory and mouthed, "Wow. That guy was *fucking* hot."

Rin's blonde locks tickled her shoulders as she shook her head in mock disgust.

"So, tell me," Gregory demanded, "what brought out the swan in our cute little duckling?"

Happy for the distraction, Rin launched into the deets of retail and salon therapy. Gregory and Jen pitched in their own tales through the ordering, the drinking, and the noshing of their exquisite meals. Having worked for years in a high-end boutique in the Northwest District, Gregory had plenty of ammunition for the best stories.

Nate slammed his whiskey, and another, and another. When it became apparent she'd be the taxi home she slid both her now freezing-cold Delilahs across the table. One for her lawyer friend and surprise best shopping buddy. One for her best girl friend who taught chemistry—of all things—at Nate's school in the burbs.

Gregory whistled. "I might need someone to walk me home after this one."

"I'd offer to do it, but I'm looking to get laid," Jen said. "And you picked the wrong team for my needs. But Zach will walk you home."

"Sure thing. Just remember, if you go in for a kiss, I like them   slow and sultry," Zach deadpanned.

Rin's side ached by the time she could breathe without an ab-clenching howl. It was the laugh they all needed to get back on level ground. Nate slid his hand under her hair and massaged her nape in easy caresses.

As the crowd faded so too did their spunk. "We're not as young as we once were, kids," Gregory said with a yawn. "Who's ready for the check?"

"I'm ready for my smooch," Zach joked.

"I'm ready for one too." Jen's head swiveled, surveilling the remaining restaurant occupants.

"You two could just help each other out," Rin suggested.

"Not drunk enough." Jen's lips pursed.

"Me neither," Zach agreed.

"While y'all work out the details of Jen's love life, I'm going to take a piss," Nate announced.

"Need a hand?" Jen asked, just drunk enough to forget herself. She covered her mouth and looked at Rin with wide eyes. "Sorry. It sounded funnier in my head."

Nate left, accustomed to their friend's episodes. "It's fine," Rin assured her.

Jen buried her face in Gregory's neck. "How about you and I split a cab?" he suggested.

"But you only live a few blocks from here," Jen whined.

While they worked out transportation, Rin seized the opportunity to talk to Zach. Of all the group, they had the least in common. But, working with Nate, he'd have an insight into his work life. "So, Zach, that health class you guys subbed for, did the teacher have her baby yet?"

"She popped the thing out a few months ago." He grinned. "I haven't had to talk venereal diseases in quite some time now."

"Maybe you should," Jen giggled.

"A doctor could explain the redness," Gregory squawked between heaving roars of laughter.

"Jesus, we need to leave before they kick us out. I could hear y'all in the bathroom." Nate sat, pulled out a hundred dollar bill, and set it on the table. "Ante up, kids."

After they worked out the bill she and Gregory walked out the restaurant arm-in-arm. "You really okay?" he asked.

Rin found her gaze searching out the scary waiter, even though she didn't want to find him. She didn't. "Just deep thinking."

"About your mom?" His strong arms tightened around her.

"No. Not my..." Rin's brain blinked out, completely on the fritz. The first line of the text flashed in her mind.

The CAL urn came back negative for human remains.

"No," she whispered. It couldn't be. The CAL urn. Her mother had been cremated after the incident. Her mother, whose name was Cara Ann Lee.

Chapter Three

On the street in front of her condo, Rin kissed Nate and tasted the spearmint of his toothpaste as opposed to last night's whiskey. "Drive safely."

"Yeah, you too, babe. Want me to give you a ride?"

"I'll stretch my legs and breathe some fresh air before I'm held captive at my desk all day."

"See you tonight." He pinched her hip and headed for his car sandwiched front and center between two sedans. After making the block several times with no luck the night before, she'd sacrificed her prime spot. Moving her Civic to a lot at the back of the block and parking his in her place seemed easier than steering his wavering steps all that way.

Nate nodded, dropped into the low-slung car, and revved the engine to life. She waved him off and started down the block. Her heels struck the concrete in angry taps. Why'd she have to be such a coward? She'd lain in the dim bedroom staring at his phone, its shiny black case gleaming in the filtered moonlight. His breathing had evened, and then the snoring began. Still she hadn't been able to make her thousand-pound arms move. Fear had held her immobile while curiosity fended off sleep.

In those long hours every possibility that paraded through her mind seemed the perfect content for a D-list Hollywood movie. The more she walked the higher her ire rose. Rin was far from helpless. It was about damn time she quit running so hard from her past that she forgot that important fact.

Her gaze darted down the street, left, and then right. Finding no sign of Nate's loudly painted red car, she spun on her camel-colored Nines and practically sprinted back to the condo.

If she didn't want to be late for work, she had fifteen minutes and she planned to make them count.

Rin slipped into the foyer, checked the street once more—for what she didn't really know—and then slipped her key into their door as quietly as she had when executing a B&E. She ducked her head into the long strap of her leather briefcase, stowed her keys in the outside pocket, and locked the door behind her. With a quick turn she assessed the living quarters, not as a proud owner, but as a thief, carefully gauging the best locations for items no one wanted found.

She opened the coat closet with only a whisper of sound and then bent low. A fancy collection of dust bunnies greeted her, tumbling with the current of air to the back corner. One by one she removed the soldier-neat line of winter boots. She shoved a hand down each, feeling for anything out of the ordinary, but came up empty. Next she caressed the wall seams and only succeeded in coating her fingers with a layer of dust.

Upper lip curled, she rearranged the shoes and made a note to clean the closet Sunday. While Nate often opted for Sunday-Sleep-Day, she caught up with laundry and household chores. Jackets next. She patted down the pockets and hems.

Nada. Determined more than deterred by the letdown, Rin unbuttoned her constricting jacket and gripped the edge of the top shelf. She stretched on tiptoes and felt around the contents.

Plastic, tall and cylindrical, cooled her touch. A pack of tennis balls. The racket she'd bought and had yet to use wedged into the back behind it. She exhaled and elongated her torso a bit more. Beneath the softly-wrapped handle, a thin, long wire piqued her attention.

Rin relaxed back and eyed the white four-top dining table, and then zeroed in on a chair. She took one step in that direction, but the recognizable boom of footsteps battered the floor just outside the painted wood of her entryway. Heart in her throat, she tucked protectively into the closet's frame and perked an ear toward the entrance. A key sounded in the lock.

"No," Nate said from outside. "I told you it's the safest place. She's at work until this evening."

"You better be right," a stern female voice retorted, her r's curling with the slightest hint of an accent.

Rin's gaze studied the closet for the best place to hide. She yanked the heels from her feet, clutched them to her chest, and stepped into Nate's knee-high boots. Silently she pulled the closet door closed and sank back into the thickness of fleece and wool, making certain the longest coats covered her knees.

With several deep breaths she steadied the hideous mixture of anger and anxiety. Her throbbing pulse roared, but not so much that she didn't hear the front door open and two treading sets of footsteps enter. Nate's and a woman's.

She'd channeled her inner delinquent for this? Sure, her blood began the slow boil that only adultery could instigate. But honestly, after the insidious trail her mind had taken last night, the thought of a little boinking, even in her own bed, deflated her balloon. Apparently the crazy text had been code for "let's screw at her place while she's at work."

"You shouldn't have contacted me," the prettily harsh voice reprimanded.

"I'm sorry, but I'm in the dark here. I didn't have a choice," Nate countered.

"There's always a choice, Harlow."

Woah, did this slut not even know his name? I mean, talk about wham-bam forgot you, man.

"And I choose to know if I should expect a bullet in the ass."

"You should always expect a bullet. It's part of the assignment. And if she's watching, she's got the crosshairs centered on your forehead, not your fit buns."

"So, you think she's behind the information breech?"

A high-pitched *snap* reverberated on the other side of the door like someone had dropped a book or slammed a heel on the hardwood. "You're not hearing me. I'm not here to soothe your shaky nerves. I'm here to catch a very dangerous woman."

What? The? Hell? Rin's waning heartbeat kicked up a notch.

"Now, Harlow, tell me, is this place bugged?" Her cadence, more than the accent, threw Rin for a loop...another loop. The woman sounded like she'd been transported from a different country and time.

"Of course. But with Rin I couldn't take the risk of cameras. It's only audio. If Lee comes snooping I need to know about it."

Well, Rin snooped all right. Damn good thing she did it quietly. Though, she got the feeling they weren't talking about her.

"If you live to see next year," the woman laughed, "you'll know that she could prance around here in your boxer briefs for hours and, if she didn't want you to, you'd never know. Don't underestimate her just because you do the same to her daughter."

Rin's knees quivered, but strength forged in the battle of life kept her from teetering.

"I've masqueraded as a doting fuck-buddy for half a year. I handle Rin just fine."

"Yes, from the looks of things you service her very well, but meeting here says you're slipping."

"I want out."

"Keep this up and you'll find the way into a body bag. Stay close to Darinda. It's been almost seventeen years, but now that she's resurrected it's possible she'll make contact. Especially if she thinks her child is in danger. Don't contact me again and don't fuck up and let her daughter get suspicious. If I need you, I'll contact you."

Dainty heels strode across the floor to the door.

"I didn't sign up for this," Nate barked.

The clack of heels ceased. "Actually, you did."

"The CIA, yeah, but not to play gigolo-in-state. We're not even supposed to operate within our borders."

"Listen here, school boy, you signed up to do whatever the hell I want you to do. Screwing a pretty young woman is hardly a hardship. I'll make sure you know what adversity is on your next assignment."

"Ma'am, I didn't mean to—"

"Take a close look," the woman spat.

Nate's in-draw of breath penetrated the dense wooden door and the swath of winter wear.

"Suffering is seven years in a North Korean prison. It's snuggling up to a drain brimming with human feces because it gives off a hint of warmth in the otherwise miserable concrete box. It's getting so familiar with pigeon torture by day that the muscles in your arms rip and knot, leaving you permanently deformed. It's denying the only scrap of food offered you in days in the hope that starvation will finally shut down your organs and take you away."

Clothing rustled, and then the front door opened. "If I hear you complain ever again, I'll fly you to hell and kick you out of the plane. Trust me, you'll curse ever opening your parachute."

The door slammed and Rin wanted nothing more than to collapse into a pile of sweat, tears, and utter confusion. But Nate seethed just outside. His ragged pants threatened to blow the house down. Her hand stung from her desperate grip on the shoes.

A deafening blow ricocheted off the wood through the tiny confines. "Fucking bitch," Nate hollered.

Rin jerked, bumping her elbow on the wall. Breath stalled in her chest and she stared, eyes swollen, in the dark, awaiting his attack. Any noise she made, Nate's continued tantrum covered. She'd never seen him rival a two-year-old for hysterics. She didn't now. But she pictured every stomp and agonized shout. And she couldn't muster one dust-mite's worth of sympathy for him.

The affection that once warmed her for the overstuffed bear of a man siphoned from her chest. A chill she shouldn't have experienced in the suffocating confines froze her marrow. The steam of lust he frenzied in her only hours ago transformed to a searing fury that rivaled the sun.

And at the same time she didn't exactly understand the cause for her anger. Was it the fact that she'd been screwing an exceptional liar for the past several months and not had an inkling about his duplicity? Was it the fact that, according to the faceless woman, her mother was alive? Was it the fact that if her mother was alive she'd never contacted her in all these years? Or was it the fact that her mother was a woman so crooked the CIA broke its own rules to try and capture her? Or did they want to kill her?

Warm tears ran down Rin's face, surprising her almost as much as the conversation she'd just overheard. Tears didn't solve anything. They were reserved for the sheltered and innocent. Not her. She billowed a slow breath through her lips in a daring attempt to harness her wild, rearing emotions.

The front door opened and slammed shut again. She should have waited a minute or ten before escaping the closet, but she couldn't breathe. Disbelief strangled her in a friendly embrace. With a quick turn of the knob, she careened from the coat coffin. The oversized boots caught on her clogs and she landed with a resounding *thud* on the cool floor, a spike wedged against the side of her boob.

Whether he was caught up in his own frustration or the timing of him exiting the building worked in choreographed perfection with her tumble, through the large open window the top of Nate's head bobbed past without a backward glance. Rin slumped to the ground, letting her cheek smash onto the wood. Well, his surveillance had certainly recorded that.

"Go fuck yourself, Nate, or whoever the hell you are, because you won't touch me." Her chest huffed on confounded outrage as her holler echoed off the glass and painted brick, smacking her eardrums. "Not ever again." The quiet snarl rasped her throat.

She pushed from the floor, sprinted to the table, shoved the dining chair toward the gaping closet door, and pounded atop it. A neat black wire lay at the back crease where the wood shelf met the plaster wall. It ran from a hole in the wall across to another hole that led to the high bookshelf facing the kitchen.

Rin peered through the living room windows and didn't see Nate or his car. She tugged one end of the wire and a small grey microphone, matching the color of her walls, slipped from the sheetrock. "Bastard," she breathed. Balling a fist, she knocked, not nearly as forcefully as she'd have liked, on the back of the closet. A hollow *thump* sounded in return.

Pulling a pen from the outside pocket of her briefcase, Rin used the instrument to pry at the joint. On the second attempt a false front gave way along with her stomach. An old-school recorder and orderly row of maybe twenty tapes nestled in the void. The ones on the left were labeled with dates and times, while the ones on the right sat in their wrappers.

Nate had a stack of these in their closet. He'd said the coaches used them to take notes on the games, which she'd never seen. Any time she'd offered, Jen had concocted a girls' night out and demanded her attendance. Nate had all but pushed her to go, citing her dislike for the sport and his long hours atop the hour it took to get to and from the school.

"You don't coach a team. You're a player in a game though."

And Jen? With her foul mouth and vulgar tendencies, a school had always seemed the most unlikely place for her to work.

"Oh my God."

Reality nearly knocked her to the floor again. Jen and Zach were her friends because they'd been Nate's friends. He "worked" with them. He'd introduced them. So, it stood to reason they worked with him. Adolescents with pocked faces and bad attitudes were the least of their concerns. They dealt in espionage and shit.

Rin leaped from the chair, thundered through the living room, past the kitchen, down the short hallway, into the bedroom, and through to the closet. She grabbed her gym bag and stuffed clothes and shoes inside, hardly taking the time to match the number of tops and bottoms. She did make sure not to take too much, so Nate wouldn't be able to tell. Crossing to his side, she grabbed a tape from the large stack. The plastic crinkled as she ripped the cover off and shoved it into her bag.

Heart chugging, Rin hurried back to the closet. She exchanged the tape in the recorder for the new one and shoved the evidence of her meddling into her trouser pocket. Sweat beaded and sucked the cotton of her button down to her skin. Carefully, she snapped several pictures with her phone before replacing the false wall, cord, and chair with the stealth of a ghost. Thinking of ghosts brought her back to her mother.

The last time she'd seen Cara Lee her blue skirt had billowed over her shapely legs as Rin watched her plummet from the roof of the Washington Golf and Country Club. Her head

shook in denial. No. She couldn't go there. Not yet.
Maybe not ever.

Rin tossed the room as neatly as she could
manage. But, if Nate was a professional, he'd likely
pay closer attention than the average Joe. She
turned up nothing of interest, but really, wasn't a
bug in your own home, the knowledge that the
person you thought you knew didn't exist and one
you thought didn't exist, might... Wasn't that
enough for one day?

Yep, sure was.

Anger forced her from the bedroom, but in a
flash of cinematic genius she returned to the
queen-sized bed and dropped to her knees. She
stabbed her arm between the mattress and box
springs. In the movies people always stashed stuff
there. The stiff fabric scraped her hand and
forearm. She felt around from the decorative pillows
to the throw at the foot of the bed, and then
switched sides. Damn him. Nothing.

She stood beside the scarred wood and
chipped paint of her antique headboard and
pondered the white coverlet and ruched gray
pillows. The sheets had been tangled on that bed a
thousand different ways the thousand different
times she and Nate had enjoyed each other's
bodies. No way in hell would she lay with him
again.

The question was, how could she get out of it
without landing a bullet between her eyes?

A tiny crack in the seam of the floor caught
her attention. Rin leaned forward and yanked the
single slat from its neat home. The hollowed-out
space in the floor nestled the smooth vinyl covering
of a passport and a neat stack of bills bound by a
teller's sleeve. With one shaky, scuffed hand, Rin
pulled them from the nook.

"Nathan Harlow," she said in a muted whisper. "I've got you, you son of a bitch."

Chapter Four

"Ms. Lee, I need the reports on Kessler and Eglin Air Force Bases by the end of the day."

Rin's gaze lifted from the endless rows and columns eating every inch of her computer screen to the starched black suit and face of her superior. In all the long hours Rin had put in at the office over the course of her short career, Shakina Morris's gorgeous ebony skin hadn't once cracked its ultra-professional veneer. Rin valued the trait, wished she had the control to mask her reactions. It would sure help if she faced Nate again.

"Hi, Mrs. Morris." She smiled. No, the woman never returned the gesture, but it didn't mean she didn't appreciate a friendly face. Rin grabbed two file folders and held them out. "I emailed the assessments maybe four minutes ago, and here are the prints along with some notes."

"Both of them?" Shakina Morris's right brow twitched.

"Yes, ma'am."

"But you came in late this morning."

"Six minutes," she nodded. "I apologize, but won't give an excuse for mismanaging my time."

"If everyone would mismanage it so well, I'd let you all take a half-day Friday." Shakina cradled the files in her arm like precious babies and sighed.

"I don't get personal with my employees for my own reasons, but are you okay?" She leaned in and whispered, "You look like you've been crying."

"Oh. I got new makeup yesterday. Maybe it's a reaction to the new chemicals," Rin lied, sticking as closely as possible to the truth.

"Right." Shakina turned to leave.

"Mrs. Morris, I have a favor to ask."

The woman stopped and swiveled on her pumps with an exaggerated exhale. "What is it?"

"I need an hour for lunch, please. My grandfather lives at the Potomac Center. When I go visit after work, he's always asleep and I don't want to disturb him." Shakina's face maintained its waxy neutrality. So, she continued, "I'll have Fort Jackson's report in your box before I leave for the day."

"I want them done correctly. Take your hour lunch and have the assessment to me by Monday."

"Thank you."

"You have my favor. Don't abuse it, Ms. Lee."

***

"Seriously, lady, go." Rin beat the steering wheel like Questlove, her straight hair probably standing on end like his did too. A white-headed woman parked at the main entrance, her extra-long, extra-wide town car congesting the lot better than a deep fried Twinkie did an artery, all so she could shoot the shit with another white-haired lady standing at the corner.

She drummed harder, falling into the words of the song to keep from falling over the steep edge of rationality. The Roots played and Quest sang.

"*I was born faceless in an oasis*
Folks disappear here and leave no traces
No family ties nigga no laces

Less than a full deck nigga no aces
Waitin' on Superman losing all patience"
The impulse to roll down the windows and blare the two ten-inch subs corroding from disuse in her trunk peaked as patience waned for answers to *WTF* was going on with her life. Lucky for her, the three cars waiting behind her, and the resident of the nursing home, the ole biddy shoved off. Rin zipped into a parking space opposite the covered walkway. In the rearview mirror, traffic poured.

She didn't think anyone had followed her. Several erratic turns and loop-d-loops saw to that as best as her amateur skills allowed. When she opened the door mid-day heat assaulted her, but the smothering humidity and blazing sun took last place on her list of concerns. She stood, looped the briefcase strap over her shoulder, locked up, and headed across the roasting concrete.

A high-pitched whine brought her up short. Good thing too. Or she'd have ended up a motorcycle pancake. A sleekly powerful BMW prowled past. The respectable machine barely blipped on her danger radar, even with the pancake possibility. The man with the capable beast between his thighs, however, pinged out her sensors on dueling fronts: a headboard-banging fuck and run-for-her-life.

His leanly muscled physique punctuated the badass-ness of distressed jeans and a threadbare baby blue T-shirt that had nothing to do with a department store and everything to do with life lived on the rugged side of humanity. Whether from the color of the shirt or the force of her reaction, Rin suddenly thought about the wildly disturbing waiter from Restaurant Barcelona.

"Luck." The name croaked from her dry throat.

The blacked-out full-face helmet the driver wore concealed his identity. The man didn't look in her direction. That stony disregard clenched her stomach. Rin wasn't conceited about her looks, but she was beautiful. For better or worse, she favored her mother as much as identical twins mirrored one another. When she crossed a street, men and women rubbernecked and catcalled way too often. But not this guy.

Rin licked her lips, clutched her bag, and did a Carrie Bradshaw dash up the sidewalk and into the building. The perfume of the infirm hung thick in the air. At least it took care of the ridiculous heat pooling between her legs. It also gave her appreciation for the energetic rattling of her heart.

"Ms. Lee?" Jeanine lifted her hands in praise. Her rose cheeks and gaping smile kept Rin from worry. She rushed from behind the tall desk. "The senator is having a great day. He recognized me twice this morning." A quick wave and even faster feet urged Rin to follow. "I tell you, it made my week. It's been a while since he's come back to us. I'm pleasantly surprised to see you, and I know he'll be overjoyed."

In spite of all the recent drama a smile arched Rin's mouth. She put her Nines to work on the linoleum, knowing she'd pay for her track-and-field training in them today and not caring. Paw-Paw came to bat for her. She'd run to West Virginia and back to see the light of recognition in his eyes.

"Senator Lee, I have a special visitor for you." Jeanine rounded the corner to her grandfather's room and stopped so abruptly Rin crashed into her back.

"I'm sorry," Rin said.

The nurse froze in place.

"What is it?" Rin asked, scared to hear the answer. She peered around Jeanine's torso. Her grandfather sat slumped to the side in a chair facing the window. "No," she cried before she could cap her emotions.

"Why don't you wait outside, Ms. Lee?"

Rin dipped below the nurse's arm and burned the skin of her knees sliding to a halt next to the desk chair. This was her chair. The place she sat during every visit to hold his hand and watch him sleep.

"Paw-Paw?" She grabbed his frail, icy hand and brought it to her cheek. A sob shook her, but she bit the awful sound back. God, but she hated old people. Old people insisted on dying and, damn it to hell, it hurt.

Jeanine placed two fingers on his carotid. "He has a pulse. A strong one." She sighed. "Senator?" Her petite hands patted his shoulder. "Senator," she hollered.

Former US Senator Cotton Lee blinked his green eyes and lifted his head as though it weighed thirty pounds. The smoke of cataracts lightened the depth of that old Irish color. "Cara?" his worn voice quavered.

"No, Paw-Paw, it's Rin."

The rumpled skin of his brow deepened its crease. He pulled his hand away gently. "I'm sorry, pretty lady. You look just like my daughter."

"I am your daughter's daughter. Your granddaughter," Rin pressed. He turned away and stared through the glass out onto a small lawn rimmed with flowers.

"I apologize for the scare, Ms. Lee." The nurse smiled. "Sit with him awhile. Talk. Maybe he'll come back. Maybe he won't. But don't give up on him."

"Never." Rin swatted at her tears and pulled a chair from the far wall.

"I'll be making rounds with the doctor soon. If you need anything, someone will be at the desk."

"Thank you." Rin forced a smile until Jeanine turned to go. "Will you please pull the door on your way?"

"Of course," she said, tugging the door in her wake.

Rin's gaze danced over her grandfather. His red hair had long since faded to a dingy white. His stout frame had narrowed with time. But what feats he'd accomplished in his day.

The People's Senator. He'd been the only senator of his time—probably ever—who didn't trade-up. Not on his house. Not on his car. Not on his wife. He'd lived in DC's Trinidad neighborhood as a speck of white lint on the sleeve of the community for years before de-segregation became a movement—in part to his efforts in politics and his district.

"Thank you, Paw-Paw. Thank you for never giving up on me." Rin shrugged off her briefcase and jacket and shoved them into the seat next to her. Then she scooted her chair a bit closer. "You may not remember me, but I know you remember Cara."

"Yes, my Cara." A grin pulled at one side of his mouth, while the damage of his stroke held the other prisoner. As if Alzheimer's wasn't enough to contend with. He turned into himself like her shaky breaths didn't rattle the gray hairs on his speckled and slightly bruised arm.

That withdrawal sliced her to the bone. Rin cradled her face in her hands and sucked long breaths in an effort to steady her tattered nerves.

"I have a confession," she whispered. When he didn't respond after an arduous minute, she continued. "I hated you. It wasn't your fault, of course, but I needed someone to blame. Someone alive." Rin wiped the drops from her chin and leaned back. "I rationalized it in my head and made you pay for my mother's and father's sins. Truth is, I'm pissed at my mom. If she hadn't screwed that man and stolen me away without telling him I even existed, he wouldn't have come for me that day.

"If he hadn't hit her and ripped me from her arms, she wouldn't have shot him." The mess of red haunted her to this day, but the look in her mother's eyes had scared her more. Desperation muddled with rage, topped with mortal fear. "If the courts had not threatened to take me away, if you hadn't insisted on a party to lighten the mood and reassure your constituents, my mom wouldn't have taken her life."

Her wet fingers covered her mouth. "Some company I am, huh? But it gets worse Paw-Paw. So much worse. You always said your daughter wouldn't take her own life, and she wouldn't leave me, unless she had business to attend. You said all this contrary to the evidence: an eye witness— that'd be me—and a pulverized body of a woman the same height, weight, age, and hair color as my mom, wearing the same clothing she wore to the party."

She scrubbed her palms down the front of her slacks. "Why would you say that to a little girl who'd just lost her mother? Why would you give hope when all it did was hurt me? I despised you for that. Sure, I said it was because you made me live in the hood with exactly one fifth of another white girl for ten square blocks. But I'd have lived in Antarctica, if I wasn't given false hope that withered and died a thousand times over in my soul."

A tiny tear trickled from the side of his eyes. "I've given up hating you. You're the only family I have. The only person on earth I can trust completely...and you can't even understand what I'm saying. But, Paw-Paw, you're not the only one who believes Cara Lee isn't dead. There are people close to me who are trying to find her and I don't think it's to catch up on old times. I think they want to hurt her."

Nothing. The senator's eyes didn't flash in recognition. In fact, a hint of drool collected at the corner of his mouth. Rin crossed the tidy room, snagged a washcloth from the bathroom, and wet it. She returned and wiped at his drooping lip.

"Versions. Everyone had their own version of the story," he rasped. "She jumped because of unrequited love. She jumped because she couldn't deal with life. She was pushed. People forced her to jump. But there are no versions to the truth. Just find the truth."

"Paw-Paw?"

"See I..." A cough drew his shoulders.

"Here." Rin grabbed the plastic cup with a lid and straw combo and held it to his mouth.

He shoved it away. "See I A," he croaked.

Realization stole her breath for several seconds. "Yes, they are CIA."

"Your mother," he heaved a breath and hacked.

"My mother...what?" she whispered.

"Your mother was..." His pruned lips firmed in a smooth, almost straight, line. "She was too brave to kill herself and too smart to be forced to do it."

She blinked. "What aren't you telling me?"

"Too much will get you hurt."

"I need to know," she begged.

"Not all of it. But some things," he admitted. "Your father was a bad man. He didn't force her, but their union," he choked on the word, "wasn't voluntary." A fat tear, and then another, slipped from her grandfather's eyes.

Rin muffled her disbelief.

"He deserved killing," Cotton Lee, a staunch opponent of the death penalty, growled the words.

"You really don't think she's dead?"

His intellect glazed.

"Why would she pretend to be dead for so long? Why does the CIA want her dead?"

Rin swallowed past a knot, but before she could form another question, Cotton Lee's gaze thinned to slits and his head shook back and forth. "My Cara. She's no longer with me. My Vanessa's gone too."

And just like that, so was he. "Paw-Paw, can you tell me about Cara? Please, a little more?"

"Not much to hold on to these days," he warbled.

She sandwiched his chilled hand between hers. "Hold on to me."

Chapter Five

The dried exoskeleton of a common housefly caught in a slender web wafted in the air current at the edge of the vent above her desk. In the three hours and fifty-five minutes that she'd watched it since lunch nothing about it had changed... While so many things about her life had hooked a u-ey and left her choking in a plume of dust and smoke.

The electronic chirp of her desk phone sent a ripple of shock through her. Rin looked at the time on her monitor and then at the phone. Damn those four minutes. She snatched the receiver.

"Department of Defense, Accounts Analysis, Darinda Lee."

"Babe," Nate's upbeat voice filtered through the line.

Her impulse control sure was getting a workout today. Instead of slamming the phone in his ear—the only benefit of having a desk phone—she strangled the hard plastic. Anger churned, but she managed to breathe through the worst of it. "Hey. You never call me at work. Is everything okay?"

"Yeah, Zach's team has a big game tomorrow night and he needs some help seeing the weakness in their defense. So, I'll be home late tonight."

"But you're a football coach, not basketball."

"Defense is defense, babe. And you're talking to the champ."

She only hoped he had a weakness she could exploit. Drilling an opponent's weak spot was the only thing that had kept her alive during junior high and high school. His overinflated ego deserved her attention. "Doesn't it take offense to win a game?"

"My offense is getting stronger."

"I'll hang out here. I have a pile of work to do."

"See you tonight."

"Whip 'em into shape," Rin said because she hoped she wouldn't see him tonight and she couldn't bring herself to say so. Not that she had much of a choice but to see him.

Alive, angry, and confused beat dead by a marathon's length.

She'd planned a mad dash to the Pentagon Library, but being in this place with eyes on her everywhere she went—even to pee—set her skin crawling. How easy would it be for Nate to get the footage and see her snooping? Besides, she knew where the best records of her mother's accident were held, and they weren't in a library.

Rin collected her briefcase and hot-footed it through the maze of cubicles, corridors, and robust security measures. When she exited the main gate on foot and made it to the bus stop in time to slip through the closing doors, the tension cramping her shoulders eased...because she left good-girl Rin at the corner.

A swipe of her SmarTrip card afforded her a back-row seat sandwiched between two young black men. Her slouch of utter exhaustion mimicked their own I-don't-give-a-shit-postures. They eyed her as though she'd been beamed from a hovering spacecraft. Rin bit the inside of her lip. "What? Never seen a white girl before?"

The guy on her left laughed.

The college athlete—she'd bet money—on her right planted his size 13 spit-shined white Dunks on the floor, leaned forward, rested his forearms on his knees, and turned his head until they were nearly eye level. "Never on the bus to our neighborhood."

"I'm older than you. So, that makes it *my* neighborhood."

"Callin' bullshit," the big guy boomed.

"Then you'll get your Dunks dirty." She smiled. "Graduated from Spingarn."

He gave a hearty laugh.

"No shit?" his friend asked with wide eyes.

"None." She swiped her hand level in the air.

"I'd have given my sac…" he coughed. "I really wanted to play there. My grandpa played for the green wave with Ollie Johnson," the big guy said.

"All-American two years in a row," Rin marveled.

"She knows her stuff," Leftie nodded.

"What are your names?" she inquired.

"He's Darius," the baller said, "and I'm Antonio."

"Nice to meet you, Darius and Antonio." She shook their hands in turn.

"I'm guessing you've moved on to bigger and better things?" Darius asked. "Don't hear tales of the elusive albino trottin' round the neighborhood."

"You know, things are better than they were when we were in junior high, but a lily white dime…" He grimaced. "No offense." Rin grinned and shook her head. "But a lady like you could attract all kinds of unwanted attention, especially at night." Antonio rubbed his expansive palm on his saggy jeans.

"Let's just say I know my way around trouble," Rin offered.

Darius's brow tightened. "What's your name?"

"Darinda, but you can call me Rin."

"You're old man Lee's granddaughter?" Antonio's head whiplashed and he looked at her through a sideways glare. "Nah. You're too soft."

"Yeah, she pretty much ran Trinidad back in the day," Darius awed.

Rin rested her head against the glass and closed her eyes against the flood of memory.

"Fuck," one of them breathed.

The bus rocked its way over potholes, jerked its way to stops, and puttered on time and again. On the fifth stop, the young men shifted and the canvas of backpacks rustled. Rin roused. "Gallaudet, huh?"

"It's not Kentucky or Arizona, but here they pay me to play a game I love." Antonio shrugged on his book bag.

"And I get to bag all the bitche... babes he doesn't have time for," Darius admitted. "It works out."

She situated her briefcase and, when the bus stopped, stood with the guys. On the street, Antonio presented his fist. "Do me a favor?" he asked.

"Depends on the favor." Rin tapped it with her own.

"Smart," Darius said, offering his clenched hand for a goodbye.

"Get out of here before dark," Antonio demanded.

"I'll do my best," Rin conceded, tapping Darius's hand. "Y'all are good boys. Stay that way."

The guys nodded. Rin bowed her head and turned away from the college entrance. She walked up the sidewalk, staring across the road at the spired steeple and American flag atop Chapel Hall until it disappeared behind an oak. On this thoroughfare the lush green trees and the cars parked beneath them lined the road. Home. A surprising smile tugged at her lips. When visiting as a little girl she raced her grandparents between trees. She'd cut innumerable swirling successions of cartwheels on their lawn.

Continuous blocks of row houses sat across from the college's wrought-iron fence, their barred windows and scum-covered brick as uninviting as ever. A few of the units boasted chic paint jobs. The bright red doors had the effect of a stop sign on thieves. It said, 'Young professional with more money than sense. A one stop shop. Come on in.' Kind of like vacant houses did.

Green wavy grass peeked from the second block's street corner—the only large plot of grass for several square blocks. Her grandparents' lawn and painted yellow house with smart black shutters began the next row of homes. Shriveled corpses of mums and some other kind of flowers cluttered window boxes on every damn window. Rin shuddered at the evidence that life left the place nearly a year ago.

Regret clouded her vision. One missed Sunday dinner was now a missed opportunity to tell her MeMe goodbye. She blinked the moisture away, kicked off her heels at the curb, and hopped over the low stone wall onto nature's carpet. Her pale polish and even paler skin contrasted against the earth. The world she lived in was ruthless concrete. She appreciated the suppleness of nature, but it was far less predictable.

She trundled through the yard. At the carport in back she brushed her feet off and slapped on her shoes. With a turn of a key in the deadbolt the ancient door groaned open. Rin hurried through the kitchen, living room, and up the stairs, ignoring the pangs of the past and its photo displays. When she reached the landing the wood shrieked under her weight. Gooseflesh stampeded over her skin. Not at the sound, but at the three closed doors that greeted her.

May. She'd been here two and a half weeks ago to clear the mail from the door slot and check on the place. And she hadn't closed the doors. Why would she? The masses of wood cut off circulating air, creating a veritable second-story oven. A temperature spike of twenty degrees should have baked the sweat from her pores. Instead, a chill clung.

"If someone's in here, now's your chance to get the fuck out," she hollered.

Nothing stirred.

Rin unwound the briefcase from across her body and hung it on the knob at the top of the banister. Then she pulled off her shoes and set them next to the bag. Without pondering the stupidity of not running out of the house, she flung the first door wide. At the foot of her grandparents' bed, scrawled in red block letters, lay the word QUESTION.

Someone could have played her like an electric guitar. That's how tight her muscles tensed at the invasion. The empty closet gaped across the room. Thankfully she'd given her grandmother's clothes away a few months ago. A cherry wood dresser stood wedged into the corner, fifties wallpaper bracketing it on each side. As opposed to an intruder. Rin glared at the word and then turned to the second door.

Mouth screwed tight, she all but ran at the second door. AND. The single blood-red word stained the white tiles of the narrow bathroom. The floral shower curtain concealed the tub's interior, while the window yawned, sending the barest wisp of a breath through the frame, rippling the nylon.

Yeah right. The unsuspecting fool heads straight for the window and *bam*, the killer leaps from the shower. Not gonna happen here.

Rin eased from the door on silent steps, grabbed her grandmother's Waterford crystal bowl filled with potpourri, slipped into the doorway, and hurled the glass at the shower curtain.

On impact, the heavy bowl billowed the fabric and then met the wall. Chunks of crystal blasted in every direction, plinking and bounding across the ceramic-lined room. Rin's heart ricocheted in her chest the same damn way. She sucked in several shaky breaths. So, no one hid in the shower.

With measured steps Rin hopped to the window and looked out. The tar roof that covered the porch didn't house a criminal either. *Question and...*

Suddenly, fear, an emotion she hadn't truly experienced in so very long, crawled into her head like a spider and spun a web so sinister she stepped toward the hallway without maneuvering through the crystal mine field.

"Son of a bitch," she hissed. She plopped on the closed toilet lid and pulled her left foot high. Red coated the pad from the tip of every toe to the cliff of her heel. She hiccuped a breath. The pain had been sharp, but not enough to draw this much blood. Unless it hit an artery.

Rin zeroed in on the point of rapidly-dulling burn. A shard of translucent crystal protruded from her low arch. She grit her teeth and pulled the piece free. The bit measured a few centimeters by a few centimeters. Not big enough to cause much damage.

She lifted her right foot and found it soaked in red too. Her gaze dropped to the muddled AND. The paint was still wet. Whoever did this hadn't done it long ago.

Her gaze flew to the hallway, what little of it she could see. It wasn't enough for her comfort. Carefully this time, Rin stood and stamped stupid toe prints across the bathroom floor. No help for it now.

Though she expected what her old bedroom would say, the word DIE written in dripping streaks of red knocked her back a step.

Question. And. Die.

Rin sprinted to the chest of drawers on the far wall from the closet and dared some asshole to jump from its closed doors. She'd channel every bit of fury she'd stored over the last five years of good living and pummel him into a bloody pulp.

Fuck. The truth had versions and so did she.

She needed to find her mother's version of the truth. Then, maybe one day, she could find the true version of herself.

At the white drawer with the pink butterfly knobs, Rin yanked. The bottom drawer gave way without the arduous heave her MeMe gave when prying the thing to stash another of her clippings. But the wooden hollow usually brimming with newspaper articles was empty.

Chapter Six

Rin slammed the door on her car and peeled out of the secure parking lot to dirty looks from the handful of guards on duty. Her finger itched to flip them double salutes, but this wasn't their fault. No, it wasn't. And she was about to give a big *fuck you* to whoever messed with her grandparents' house and took her clippings.

She'd never wanted them. That hadn't stopped her MeMe from filing them away until the day Rin needed them. Well, damn it all, today was the day. She broke several traffic laws in her fit to get to the nearest hospital.

The thousands of questions pinging around her head would find answers, despite—hell—in spite of the threat. She'd stared down a gang and let them beat her into the ground as part of some screwed up ritual. And not much menaced her since. Some kindergarten finger paint wouldn't.

When she wheeled into a parking space on the third level of the dank parking structure her tires squealed. She stuffed her phone, all the cash she had in her wallet, and her license into various pockets of her slacks, and then patted the tape in her front pocket for reassurance. If a bullet or goon took her out before she found answers, she wanted the world to know something was amiss. But if these guys were professionals, they'd think to check her pockets. So, she stuffed the tape into her bra and got out. The humidity climbed with the temperature. She shed her suit jacket for the sleeveless shell underneath and prayed too many sweat marks didn't show in the white silk.

Rin clacked her way inside to the bank of elevators on heels she'd surely wear to the nub by the end of the day. The stench of sickness and sterility melded in her nostrils, rivaling that of the nursing home in putridness. She dodged a gurney exiting the center car. A young man dressed in scrubs carted an unconscious old lady with an array of IV bags swinging at the top of a metal rod.

"The morgue?" Rin demanded with a feigned air of authority.

"Take this to the ground level, exit left, past the chapel and waiting room, hook a right at the next hallway, detective sign-in is at the desk on the left." The guy rattled the instructions with his gaze centered on her breasts.

Ha! Her a cop? She'd spent loads of time in a police cruiser...behind the metal divide. "Thanks," she offered with a sarcastic bite, before stepping onto the vacant elevator. He shuffled on without a reply. The doors closed and the car lurched toward the sky. "Damn." Rin folded her arms and waited.

At the twelfth-freaking-floor the car finally changed direction until the elevator halted for passengers on the ninth floor, and eight, and sixth. She wedged into the corner and tapped the fingers of her right hand against her arm. The surging adrenaline upped the tempo to a frantic pace.

"Jesse, stop," a mother, with a nondescript toddler on her hip and a little boy at perfect elbow-whacking height, chided the oldest. "That's driving me nuts." The boy, bless his heart, stood with nothing more than a pouty slouch, which exaggerated at the unfounded accusation.

Rin cut the kid a break and ceased the incessant drumming.

"Thank you," the mom breathed. The kid threw up his arms.

The mass of bodies shuffled off the elevator on the ground floor, but all veered to the right toward the cafeteria, gift shop, and main entrance. Rin rushed in the opposite direction down a narrower corridor so stark-white it made her look tanned.   She bobbed and weaved through the guy's instructions. The closer she came to her destination, the colder the air grew.

A portly fellow with sweat beaded across his brow despite the sub-zero temperatures sat behind a desk next to the door labeled 'Morgue'. Rin pasted on her sweet-as-sugar smile, which had worked magic on many unsuspecting marks back in the day. She draped her forearm across the high countertop of the station and leaned in, boobs first. "Hi, Rusty," she said, scoring his name from the badge clipped to his royal-blue scrubs' pocket.

He gave a jerky nod and a wave of uncertainty bathed her. She looked around and not a soul milled or hustled about. Sure, her boyfriend, the CIA...agent...operative...whatever the hell they called them, could kill her at any minute, but so too could this big, funny-acting slab of beef and there wasn't anyone around to see it. Hell, he worked in a morgue for Christ's sake.

"I'm working on my thesis," Rin lied smoothly. "It's about the ecological benefits of natural burial over embalming and cremation. I'd love to talk with your resident medical examiner or pathologist."

"We don't staff a medical examiner and our pathologist doesn't come in for a few more hours." He swiped at the moisture now dripping from his forehead. "But I'm a diener. I might be able to answer some of your questions. I can even lend you a few books." He coughed. "I'm studying to be a pathologist."

Wariness caviled with the need for answers. "Thank you, Rusty. I'd appreciate any help. Can you tell me the order of death to burial for cremation? Like the body, where is it taken? Is it left anywhere unattended before or after incineration?"

Rusty's gaze narrowed on his feet. "Sure, there's a hospital procedure guide for cremation in the back, even though the hospital doesn't perform them. We release the bodies to the funeral homes for burial prep. If you'd..." He looked at his feet again and squinted. "If you'll head through those double doors. I'll get someone to man the desk and I'll show you what I have."

"Thanks." She stepped toward the doors he pointed to, trying to see behind the wide wall of desk. Filing cabinets and the width of the desk itself shielded Rusty's lower half from view. Maybe she'd caught him whacking off or reading a Cosmo. She dismissed the alarm bells because everything in her life set them off right now.

Rin pushed past one of the heavy doors and stopped so abruptly the thing nearly whacked her in the butt. She'd expected an office or hallway. Instead, blinding fluorescent fixtures illuminated a metal table. Grating covered the top, making it look like an extra-large colander. A faucet with one of those salon hair-washing attachments protruded from one end. What looked to be a football punt stand sat in the center of the table just beneath the spigot.

On the right side of the room a bank of three-foot by three-foot silver-faced cooler doors lined the wall fifteen deep. The only thing keeping her inside the house of horrors was that the bodies were stowed safely behind those secure doors and not under a flimsy sheet with their feet hanging out. She shuddered and stepped toward the rows of books stacked neatly on shelves over a counter that ran the length opposite the body-wall.

Odorous chemicals she never wanted to identify or smell again stung her nostrils. Rin rubbed the end of her nose and perused the titles littering the work space. *Forensic Pathology: Principles and Practices. Medicollegical Investigation of Death. Gunshot Wounds: Practical Aspects of Firearms, Ballistics, and Forensic Techniques.* Neon sticky notes and dog-eared pages feathered the books. At least Rusty wasn't kidding about studying. Her gaze lifted to the shelf and scanned for the word 'cremation'.

All this and more polluted the Internet, but she wanted concise information from a source that couldn't be traced. Thinking of her source, she wondered what the hell was taking him so long. Only not for long. Her vision alighted on a text with the word she was searching for. She snagged a pen from the desk and reached for the book.

A click pierced the quiet. The blindingly bright room turned pitch black. Books, the freaky autopsy table, and the wall-o-corpses, and every other weird thing in between, disappeared in a sea of syrupy black. Rin pinched her eyes shut and slammed her hand over her mouth, fighting the urge to scream. This wasn't happenstance. Strain as she might, no sound other than the drone from the air vents filled the large square room. But she sensed a presence. To her dread, it wasn't a ghost.

The power of the human wraith—or just maybe the power of her overactive imagination— drove her toward the gruesome table in the middle of the room. If she could get it between her and whoever stalked her in the eclipse of artificial light, she could dodge them and make it to the door. Rin lowered her hand for balance, cinched her grip on the pen in her other hand, and ventured one easy step at a time.

Three down. Her foot quaked on the fourth step. She reached out, feeling for the cold metal. Her open palm met something hard and hot under the thin cotton of a T-shirt.

Rin sucked a year's supply of oxygen from the room. She pitched left and ran hard, slipping on the polished floor. The rumble of feet in pursuit should have echoed in the space, but only a whisper rippled the air a moment before the steely iron of hands scorched their way down her arm and banded her wrists.

She teetered on heels, but the restraints kept her from plummeting to the floor. Her attacker raised both her arms high over her head in one large hand and bound her waist with a merciless forearm. The instinct to fight back lay somewhere in the corner of her mind huddled in a terrified lump. All the spit had apparently evaporated from her mouth. She couldn't swallow, let alone scream.

The metal wall came hard and fast. Her cheek ground against the raised edge of one of the body lockers. His body blanketed her own as hard and immovable as the metal to her front, only hot. No way was this soft-middled Rusty.

There hadn't been much doubt about the gender of her attacker, but now she knew without a doubt. The hard ridge of a—respectably large, in any other situation—cock pillowed into the cushion of her ass cheek. So, it wasn't Nate.

Wits returning, Rin struggled for freedom. She used the wall as leverage and shoved backward, only managing to stroke him far too intimately. Yanking her arms, his grip tightened impossibly. Next, she levered her heel and tried to stomp a hole through his foot. Strong legs bound her thighs to the wall, making her efforts futile at best and completely draining at worst.

Sweat slicked her skin. She panted in rage and exhaustion. He didn't seem the least hindered with her shenanigans. The moment she stilled, his arm left her middle. A locker to her immediate right popped open. It coursed a breeze over her torso and the putrid smell of death and ammonia tripled.

She turned her face away and gagged. A metal-on-metal squeak resonated in the four walls. He pulled her right hand from above her head. Rin tried to break free, but this guy was immovable. He knew just how to pin her to make her useless in defending herself. "Fuck you," she growled.

"Do you want to end up on a slab like this guy?" he asked.

Her world spun more than it had all day, and that said something. She'd heard the honeyed voice, now growling in her ear, before.

Luck.

"Answer me." He pressed her hand down to the cold, dead body. "Do you want to join this bastard?"

Rin cringed away, but moved nowhere. He shifted them closer to the body. "No. No!" She hollered the answer.

He regrouped her hand in his and yanked the hem of her shirt from her pants.   She stopped breathing. His hand slid up her side and across her bra. Two hot fingers dipped between her breasts and removed from the intimate spot the tape she'd taken from Nate's recorder.

"Then don't go down this path. It will get you killed," he ordered.

"By you or Nate?"

The warmth cocooning her in the frigid room lifted. She didn't hear the whisper of receding footsteps, but just like that he was gone. The threatening presence vanished. In a lightning flash, the lights popped on.

Rin's gaze fell on a thin, white body bag. She jerked back, her eyes sweeping the rest of the room. No one, but her and the person on ice.

She sprinted on wobbly feet toward the door and burst through to the corridor. Luck was nowhere in sight, but Rusty sat in his chair where she'd last seen him. He hunched over his desk with his head resting atop both his arms.

Let him be alive. Let him be alive.

The chant went round and round in her mind as she stepped closer to the guy and extended two fingers. She pressed them to his neck. "Oh, thank you."

Chapter Seven

Rin zipped through a shower, spending most of her time scrubbing the soles of her feet. She dressed in shorts and a billowy top before drying her hair, which never happened. But she'd rather join the guy in the morgue than have Nate even try to put his hands on her. It hadn't been him in that horrifying place. Yet, he'd started this whole train rolling down a track she didn't favor one little bit.

She slapped on makeup for something to do while she waited. Was this all worth it to get her mother back or was she stupid for even entertaining the idea that the woman still existed beyond some cooked-up bones? Rin tossed the hair dryer under the cabinet and smiled at the crash it made.

The thought of food bubbled her stomach. So, she stomped to the living room, flopped onto the sofa, and grabbed the Vogue from the coffee table. After twenty minutes of staring at the cover, a key sounded in the lock.

"Hey, babe." Nate dragged his wide-load frame through the door as though he'd spent the day coaching an NFL training camp. The white salt of long-dried sweat rings stained his high school logo emblazoned T-shirt. His gym bag, which held who knew what, slumped his shoulders to one side.

Rin unfurled her legs from beneath her, sat straight, and gathered her courage. "Nope. Don't babe me. Not ever again."

Nate drew to an easy halt inside the door. He let the bag slide to the floor and tilted his head toward her with a palliative hand drawn, palm up. "What'd I do this time or forget to do? It's not our anniversary, unless you do that half-anniversary bullshit. Then I missed it by a little. Babe." He bit his cheek. "I'm sorry I forgot."

"This isn't about an anniversary, Nate."

"Then wanna tell me what it *is* about?" He stretched his arms wide. "I'm at a loss."

Rin stood more confidently than she had in a while. "Oh, you know what I'm talking about. You just didn't know that I knew. But I'm not stupid. Not near as fucking senseless as you are." She slammed the piece of paper she'd hidden in the magazine down on the wooden coffee table between them, and then she folded her arms.

He closed and locked the door. His deliberate movements zinged a chill up her spine. She shook it off. Almost there. Almost home free.

"What is it?" Nate asked before turning. He maintained a neutral mask, but the edges cracked in the bulging vein in his neck and the grinding of his jaw.

"Why don't you ask your girlfriend?" Rin spat.

"I did."

"Nope. Me," she said, pointing at her chest, "not your girlfriend." She made a deliberate show of peering at the paper. "Jen, on the other hand, has— skillfully from the sound of things—mastered that art."

"Where'd you get that?" he barked.

"Wrong question," she breathed through her teeth. "You need to ask, 'How long do I have to get my shit out of your house before you give it to the homeless, Rin?'"

"I'm not cheating on you." He spread his feet and hands in an I-have-nothing-to-hide gesture.

"Said every cheater in the history of cheaters."

"Someone's fucking with us. Trying to break us up."

"Oh, Jen is fucking with you all right, shoving that note under the door, but she's not screwing me and neither are you. Ever again. I'll pack your stuff and leave it in the hallway tomorrow." She stormed through the apartment, held her breath, and prayed he didn't follow.

When she crossed the threshold of her bedroom she slammed the door and depressed the measly lock. Fists, high in the air, pumped as though she'd just performed on Broadway and killed it. Because Jen and all her slutty ways had bloomed in Rin's mind in a moment of desperation. She needed Nate out of her life without him suspecting any ill-gained knowledge on her part.

She'd scribbled the note in bubbly girl-script she hadn't employed since elementary school and hopped in the shower, hoping she got out before he arrived, but setting the stage for any eventuality.

The chorus of George Michael's *Freedom* played in her head, which surprised her. She didn't know her soul's musical database stored anything like that.

Sleep seemed like the next step in her scheme. Despite the sun shining its orangey-red rays in the sky outside her window, the day's events had drained her for anything else. Since the body incident, eating hit last on her list of things to do.

Nate's concussive beating on the door jarred that thought right out of her head. "Open the door, Rin. We need to talk."

"There's nothing to talk about. Please leave."

"I'm not going anywhere," he growled.

"Tell that to the cops, dip-shit."

Boom!

The wood frame splintered. Layers of paint gave way, becoming projectiles in the room. The door swung open, hit the wall, and bounded back again.

Rin sprinted for the closet, but a biting hand gnashed at her hip. She teetered off balance and careened into the bathroom countertop. A sharp pain seized her side. She gripped the faucet to stay upright, so differently than she had just yesterday.

Her heart beat in her throat, restricting her panted breaths. She grabbed the glass jar candle and heaved it with everything she had. Too damn bad she didn't aim worth a damn. The thing sailed past Nate and thudded onto the floor three feet to his left without bothering to shatter.

"Damn you, Rin." His face reddened like a bull as he stalked her way. "If I have to, I'll beat you into submission."

"You'll have to kill me," she choked.

"I can do that too." The cold glint in his eyes made so much sense in that moment. "You'll be mine or you'll be dead."

She could take a beating, but she'd never received one from someone as big as Nate. One punch in the right place would end her. If she didn't fight at least enough to get away, she'd die today.

His hand wound into her hair and he positioned her to face the mirror. "I want you to watch closely as I make this pretty face an ugly mess no man in his right mind would want."

His other hand wound up for a punch. Rin readied her leg for a heel to the groin. He released, but impact never collided with her cheek. She heard it though, a resounding *whack*. But she didn't feel it. Instead her scalp seared as her head was yanked nearly off her shoulders. She stumbled back, but clung to the countertop.

Nate sailed back and slammed into the wall between the shower and closet. He snarled at something across the room, released what was left of her hair, and hopped up. "I knew you were behind it. I saw you for what you were yesterday. The only thing that saved your life was the crowd."

Rin gripped her skull and cut her gaze toward the person he talked to. Luck stood, fists clenched, but otherwise completely cool-as-Ice-Cube, his gaze zeroed on Nate. It had been him at the morgue. The waiter's get-up was gone, but the striking blue eyes, thick lips, and commendable physique remained.

"Actually, Rin's much more cunning than you give her credit for. And I'll die one day, but not by your hand." Luck smiled, a cold, sinister mockery of the gesture's natural intent.

Nate grabbed her shoulder. She tried to pry his hand off, but his grip only tightened. Rin rammed her knee into his rib and followed it with an upper-cut that jolted every bone in the extremity. He hardly grunted. His fat hand wrapped around her throat and he lifted.

"Just like you to take advantage of those unable to defend themselves," Luck taunted. "When you get done screwing around, I'll be happy to end you with my bare hands, Harlow."

"Get in the shower and don't come out until I'm done." Nate shoved her toward the toilet without a glance in her direction.

Rin's hand squeaked across the closed lid. She stumbled forward, catching herself before she flew headfirst into the shower stall. Behind her, the *thwack* of flesh meeting flesh clenched her stomach. Her head snapped around to see what the hell the two beasts were doing to each other. The room spun farther than she turned. She grabbed either side of the doorframe for several seconds before things came into grizzly focus.

Nate's fists whaled Luck's ribs with one deft blow after another. Only the top of the man's floppy blond hair showed from his elbows-down, chin-low hunch. How much more could he take? Nate outweighed him by twenty or more pounds of bulky muscle. Talk about a non-rescue.

She ran to the closet, using the wall for balance, since Nate had knocked—or yanked—hers for a loop. On the bastard's side of the closet she pulled his toolbox from a low shelf and flipped it open.

Her hand wrapped around the silicone end of a heavy hammer. The last time she used a common household item to pummel someone she'd almost traded her freedom for bars and an orange jumpsuit. She grabbed her revolting belly and stood with the heavy weight of the tool and broken promises. But she couldn't let Nate, or Nathan, or whoever, kill the guy who'd saved her from a sure beating.

Luck's head still hung low, but now he rocked almost imperceptibly from side to side. Deciding to aim for a less vital organ than the head, Rin stayed back and probed for the best plan of attack.

Like in the morgue when Luck had flipped the switch from light to dark, he did it again. He exploded from his crouch, hooked Nate's forearm with his own, and yanked sky-high. His other hand landed a blow that snapped Nate's neck back like a head-on collision. Luck disengaged, loosening his shoulders as he waited for the other man to recover.

Nate scrubbed his face and hopped back and forth on the balls of his feet. He took gentle forays into the strike zone, flinging a jab haphazardly. Rin covered her mouth with her hand. She had no love for Nate, not even when they dated, but pussy-footing about like that was going to cost him dearly. And as much as she'd like to see the fall-out, she'd hate it almost as much. What Luck lacked in bulk he more than made up for in cool calculation and precision enforcement. And the big guy—

A cluster of punches in and around the gut, best she could tell, shoved Nate out of the fight. Once. Twice. The third time he roared so loudly she jumped. Then he charged, shoulders forward, head down, for Luck's torso. The lean stranger jumped. He cocked his elbow and then fired the point of his bone down straight onto the crown of Nate's head.

Nate's hefty frame hit the ground in an unconscious heap.

The whole tangle took less than a minute, but Rin would have sworn she'd watched it for an hour. Every strike and blow sealed in her brain on ultraslow motion.

Luck stepped over Nate and held out his hand.

Chapter Eight

"Can't follow simple instructions, can you?"

Rin Lee's skinny arms hoisted into the air. Her pretty mouth was screwed into a grimace. The small-but-impressive muscles in her arms flexed and she tossed the hammer like a lumberjack did a hatchet. It arched high and wide, missing him by several feet. It bounced before somersaulting on the cushy bedding.

"Damn good thing you can't aim either," he goaded.

Her deep blue eyes lasered as if she'd like nothing more than to obliterate him with the glare.

"We need to go." He offered his hand again, but the stubborn woman didn't budge. "They gave him the kill order. When he doesn't check in they'll send backup."

"You killed him?" The furrow in her brow appeared more surprised than forlorn.

"No, but he'll be out for a while."

He flicked his wrist to hurry her along. Desired effect unattained.

She cocked a hip and planted her hands on each lopsided one. "Who are you?"

"Luck." He smiled.

"Seriously." Her voice layered with a rumble.

"Doesn't get more serious than that. Now, I'm going. You can come or stay. The choice is yours. If you stay though, you might want to get straight with the Lord."

"How do I know you're the good guy?" she huffed.

"Oh, I'm definitely not the good guy, but I won't kill you or let anyone else off you either."

"Where are we going? What's going on? Why does the CI—"

Movement in the apartment above set him off. He lunged forward, grabbed her wrist, and towed her toward the bedroom door.

"I thought it was my choice."

"Who the hell would choose to die? You don't have some debilitating disease you're keeping secret, do you?"

Her wrist twisted in his grip. "I need my shoes."

"Women," he breathed and released her.

She hustled to the closet. Three seconds later she exited with sandals, which were hardly shoes in his book, and a small duffle overflowing with clothes. In her golden-lace shorty-shorts, flowing white top, and sandals, she looked more Barbie than juvenile delinquent. And damn him to the underworld, his body reacted to her in both looks.

"We're walking out of here casually. Two crazy kids on a first date. Not a hurry in the world. If I run though, you'd better keep up."

"Ooh, I can't wait until the second date. What are we going to do, mug a nun?"

"Come on." He interlaced their fingers and headed for the front of the condo. "Your hands are freezing." He chafed them with his other hand.

"I'm sorry. Someone scared the life out of me in a fucking morgue." As their shoes hit the sidewalk she whispered the last two words.

"Shhh." He slowed and turned toward her. Wisps of her long white-blonde hair caught in the breeze. He stroked his fingers over her sharp jaw and glided them gently to her scalp. Her breath hitched on her parted lips, so thin he'd have to take extra care not to bruise them, if he ever kissed her —which he wouldn't. "There's a white truck half a block up. If they pursue, you better hold on tight."

Success. He'd stunned her into silence and gotten a good look at the truck. The exterior gleamed with a squeaky clean shine. They should have flashed a neon, 'Sup, we're here' sign above it.

When Nate had his fat hand around Rin's throat Luck's heart had almost clamored out of his chest. The sight of the truck hardly ranked a quarter-beat increase. Two more steps brought them to the edge of the sidewalk and his bike. He pulled the extra helmet from the mesh netting at the back. "Trade you."

"It was you at the nursing home." She shoved the bag at his middle with extra force. "You almost ran me over."

"Your definition of almost needs some work." He secured the bag under the netting, climbed on, and started the engine. "Phone." He patted his palm.

Rin, helmet already obscuring her face, kicked a leg over, and then smacked a case-less white iPhone onto his hand.

The bike could carry two, but it didn't leave much room for modesty, which wasn't an issue for him. Her inner thighs cupped his ass, scorching him through his jeans. Her small breasts plastered against his back. She wrapped both arms around his torso and clung with total abandon, not fear.

He tossed the phone into the road and took off like a shot in the opposite direction of the truck and the one-way traffic. The sleek device disintegrated under his wheels.

Rin poked him in the kidney, and then her fingers tapped his abs. She held up one finger and then gestured it the other way. A smile tugged at his lips. He grabbed her hand, placed it on his chest, patted it, and then gunned the engine straight ahead.

He weaved and looped, backtracked, and did it again in a different pattern through DC, making certain no one followed him. Over the course of the ride Rin's grip relaxed. She moved with him into the turns, their bodies in perfect sync and balance over the machine. By the time he turned onto the narrow alley on the north side of downtown DC and pressed the button for the single garage door, her fingers had mapped the entirety of his chest and abdomen. And he'd bet his bike she had no idea she'd been doing it. Otherwise, she'd have kept her hands still and not stoked desire that had no right to exist in the first place.

The garage door rumbled closed behind them. Luck crept past the inconspicuous sedan and parked next to the flashy ride in the skinny spot of the small garage reserved for the motorcycle. He shut off the engine, kicked the stand, and tugged off his helmet.

He bowed his head and stood, avoiding the architectural beam that jutted over the space. "Watch your head."

"What?" Rin yanked off her helmet. With a sassy shake, her hair fanned in all directions before settling in neat lines about her shoulders...and breasts.

Damn it.

He coughed and pointed. "The concrete buttress. Watch your head."

She chewed the inside of her cheek and gave a nod.

Luck retrieved her bag and started for the stairs. Her flat sandals scuttled across the floor and then thumped on the metal steps quick enough to keep pace. The opaque glass lining the staircase gave off the only light, which dwindled with the sun. At the top of the second flight he hooked a right through a large rusted cargo door.

"What are we doing in a haunted building?"

"Scaring everyone else away, I hope." He stopped at the door and ushered her into the room with both hands.

"One freaky, pitch black room a day is my quota, thanks." She stalled at the threshold.

"This is supposed to be a vacant building. Light kinda' gives it away."

"You may have bat-vision, but I don't."

He tugged her forward by the wrist and immediately regretted touching her again. His entire body roared with awareness. Two deep breaths stemmed the worst of it. But man. He placed her hand on his shoulder…as far away from his groin as he could get her touch. "Follow my steps and you won't trip over any corpses."

"Not funny." Her hot breath tickled his ear.

He shoved at the heavy rolling door. The metal groaned and slowly gave under the force. The thing should have skied into place with the amount of times he'd opened and closed it over the last year. They walked along with the oversized sliding door that made him think of old world castles and city gates.

The narrower the gap the darker the room became. The darker the room, the closer Rin's body came to his own. Her palm splayed over his lat and worked its way up his collar. When the metal latch *clanged* into place her grip tightened on his shirt, constricting the fabric around his neck. That he could live with. The feel of her cool fingers at his nape, he could not.

This animalistic attraction—his hard-on— were not in the job description.

Luck cleared the distance to the breaker in three quick strides, more than ready to be away from her. He flipped the lever and the lights flickered to a dull glow.

"Yeah, this isn't creepy at all."

"Give it a minute."

"I've given you about all the minutes I can without answers," she snapped. "Where are we?"

"DC." The sodium bulbs' brightness grew in slow degrees, alighting Rin's eyes, high cheekbones, and petite nose. He pried her hand from his collar and stepped back.

"Is this where you live?"

"For now."

Her hands tensed to blades. "Who are you?" A warning rasp layered her voice.

"I've told you. Luck."

"Fuck Luck. I need a little more to go on than that." She fisted a hank of hair and tugged at the roots. "Why do I even ask? It's not like I'd know the truth if it slapped me in the face. I didn't even know Nate was anything more than..."

"My name is Damien Luck, not that it matters. I'm nobody to anybody. And anyone who ever knew me called me No Luck."

Rin rubbed her lips together, tilted her head, and contemplated him. She swallowed and deliberated some more. "You're apparently something to me."

"Your watchdog."

"Why'd people call you No Luck?"

The need to slink into the shadows niggled. Anger at the unwanted feelings helped shrug off the past. No more hiding. These days he faced his fears head on. "It's a sob story neither of us have the time or inclination for."

"Fine. Then tell me what the fuck is going on."

"I have some questions for you. When I warned you not to ask questions, why couldn't you listen? Why couldn't you just let it ride for a few months?"

Rage narrowed Rin's eyes to black slits in the dim room. "A few months? Screw you. Why don't you go fuck someone for a month who's only there for reconnaissance?"

"I have."

"Well, I like a good bang as much as the next person—"

"I'd say you like it more," he spat, unable to stop himself.

Rin coiled on him like a viper. "I'm not a vindictive whore. And you're right, you're nothing to me."

She ran like she'd run for her life before. Knees up and shoulders back, her arms swung in rapid pendulums. Rin rammed against the metal. The tinny repercussion made its round in the large room. Her slender hands encompassed the latch. A grunt sounded her efforts, while the veins in her arms swelled to the surface of her pale porcelain skin. She shoved in the opposite direction, but neither move freed the door.

Careful not to touch her, Luck bracketed her body with his hands. Her shoulders expanded on deep breaths. Her head bowed, resting against the corroded surface. For more than a minute she evened out her breathing in the half-huddled position.

He wasn't dumb enough to think she was anywhere near done. He guessed she was trying to work an escape in her wily little mind. Only she'd figure out there was only one scenario in which she'd live to see the end.

"Son of a bitch." She kicked the door and turned on him. "I hate you."

"Good. There's no room for love or even a good tumble in this cluster."

Chapter Nine

Rin's feet throbbed, and she wore flats for-the-love. She struggled to ignore the harder than stone surface she paced and the confounding man kicked back on the bed as though the Redskins led a game by seventeen points. Too bad the walls were bare except for one corner, where a column of rustic wood with bolts protruding on either side covered a small portion of the bare masonry. She'd begun to think of it as art over the last five hours.

What the hell else could she think about without going straightjacket-crazy? She'd formulated and nixed about forty different plans of escape. She'd tried to calculate where he fit into the puzzle the day had brought. She'd tried reasoning with him. None of it had worked. Ignoring him and the entire problem seemed the only viable option.

She plodded her worn path along the far wall, leaving as much distance between them as possible. Being close to him intoxicated her body and warped her mind in such a way that when he said they couldn't screw like primal beasts the words hurt. How messed up was that—on so many levels?

How had she ever felt a connection to him at that stupid bus stop?

Luck possessed a seductive magnetism that pulled her without trying. If the creator suddenly decided to take four points off his sexy-looks ranking, but let him keep the swagger and confidence, he'd still be the most dangerously alluring man she'd ever seen. And yet, he acted as if he didn't see her as a woman at all.

Most men guided her along with a hand on her back or chanced skin-to-skin contact at any opportunity. Luck kept his hands off. Way off. And that was a good thing. If only she'd believe it.

He popped off the rumpled sheets and sauntered to the kitchenette. She wondered how exactly they'd gotten so disheveled. Was he a fitful sleeper or did he have company last night and never quite make it to sleep?

Rin scrubbed a hand over her face, turned, and headed in the opposite direction from the small oven and big pain in the ass. Besides the unmade bed and interesting raw finish on the walls, things had their places.

Okay, there wasn't much in the way of furniture. The huge bed took up half of the far wall. Not really, but it seemed to. A massive chest lay at its feet. Its padlock kept her from exploring further. The sink, oven, hand-full of cabinets, and medium-sized refrigerator rested on the wall to its right. Directly in front of it, almost in the middle of the floor, stood a large dining table capable of seating eight, if only there were more than the four chairs that rimmed it.

The immovable door forced Rin to turn back. She couldn't help but watch Luck plate two slices of pizza and set it on her side of the table. Tactically, he retreated to the edge of the bed, where he propped a hip. He hiked a foot to the end of the sturdy chest, rested a lean forearm on his knee, and eyed her.

She looked away.

"Anyone who can ignore Pete's for four hours running is a stronger person than me."

Her stomach gurgled, pleading for just a bit of the cheese he kept gooey and melted by returning it to the warm oven every time she neglected the offering. But she'd starve before she ate anything he presented unless it was freedom.

"Chinese doesn't tempt you. I know this stuff does, but you stubborn fool woman won't even take a bite. You have to be thirsty."

Without asking permission her gaze sought the glass brimming with water. She swallowed past the dehydration and kept walking.

"What do you like to eat?"

"It doesn't matter. Prisoners don't get to pick their meals." She gnawed at her lower lip, irritated with herself for speaking.

"You're not a prisoner."

Rin stopped and wheeled on him. "Then. Let. Me. Go."

His thumb rubbed back and forth over his mouth, scraping the edge of stubble so light she couldn't see it from this distance.

"Right." She turned away and continued putting one foot in front of the other.

Her legs went numb maybe twenty minutes after that and then cramped about forty or so minutes later. She judged the time by the number of laps she made. Misery loved company. That was the saying. And it must. Luck's furrowed brow creased deeper with each turn. The expression gave her odd comfort. It meant he wasn't as unfeeling as she thought.

He rose from the bed and headed for the table, but he crossed the centerline and aimed in her direction. Rin braced for a forcible halt to her pacing, but he fell in silent step beside her.

For more than thirty laps they maintained a steady gate, one beside the other. Damn him and her too, but the solidity of his presence supported her weary frame. His shoulders stood nearly a foot taller than hers. His natural stride almost doubled hers, but he measured his steps to match her smaller ones. The comfort she took in his protection peaked her ire once more.

"What are you doing?" she snapped.

"Being as ridiculous as you are."

"To hell with you."

"You're making this ten times more difficult than it has to be." His hand encompassed her upper arm and urged her to stop. He stepped in her path and then lowered his gaze to hers. "Just eat, sleep, play crossword puzzles. You'll be out of here in a couple of weeks."

"Weeks! I have a job and a home. I can't just disappear for weeks without losing everything I've worked for."

"Or you could keep down this path and I'll tranq you and insert a feeding tube." He shrugged.

That nonchalant gesture pitched her over the edge. Rin lunged for his throat. Fueled by confusion and rage she pitched them toward the floor. They landed with a *thud* that hardly registered in the haze of red fury.

He banded her hands in each of his. Her fingernails sank into his skin as she fought for freedom. The room pivoted. Cold concrete met her bare skin where her shirt hiked in the back. She kneed what she hoped was his groin, but his heavy legs constricted her own.

She strained against the hold, but his weight settled firmly over her. His impressive erection nestled perfectly at the junction of her hips. She wanted to writhe with him entrenched fully inside her. To forget everything and lose herself in him. And she hated herself for it.

He held his face far enough away that she couldn't slam her head into the bridge of his nose. But that gaze bore into hers.

"What," she spat, "are you going to rape me?"

Centimeter by slow centimeter, Luck lowered his head, his eyes searching hers all the while. She bided her time and then wrenched her head forward. Their foreheads connected with a dull *thump.* He'd seen it coming and backed away enough that stars didn't cloud her vision. He shoved forward, driving her head to the floor. Struggle though she did, her head sank under his force.

"I'm not going to hurt you, Rin Bird."

The world stilled for just a moment and everyone joined in a collective gasp. Or, at least, they should have. The air in her body thinned. If she'd been standing she'd have surely hit the deck in a woozy heap.

"How do you know that name?" She hardly recognized her thick, wet voice.

Luck's strong jaw flexed and his chest expanded against her.

"How?" The tears spilled from her eyes. She hated every one of them. "The only person who ever called me that... I watched her take a dive off the side of a building a lifetime ago."

Chapter Ten

Luck had never failed a mission. He knew his limits. Knew collateral damage was part of the game. Knew when to abandon the rules to see it through to the end. This fierce woman's tears slammed him into a wall he never saw coming. It slashed his insides like nothing else he'd ever seen, because all those missions had only been prep for this one.

In all his sanctioned stalking, in over a year of following Rin around, he'd never once seen her cry. Never once seen anything but a hellcat through the lens of his scope. If he'd allowed her to continue sprinting down the path she'd set for herself, she'd have killed herself or him in the battle, and that was unacceptable.

"She sent me to keep you safe," he whispered.

"No." A wail shook her. Tears puddled in her bloodshot eyes and streamed down the side of her face. "She's dead." Rin clenched her lids shut. Her head shook so violently that he'd swear she was possessed by the ghost of her mother—or perhaps the demons of her mother's past. "She's dead. I don't care what Nate said. I don't care..." She heaved a breath and choked. "I heard her body hit the ground."

The bowstring tension snapped and she fell lax, hiccupping. Careful to keep his crushing weight off her, Luck released her hands and caged her body with his own. Her tiny hands wedged between them. She draped her arms around her middle, hugging herself.

How many times had he done that as a child? An ache split him. The sudden and blatant need to protect her that took hold had nothing to do with his job. It sealed the wound and gave him purpose.

He laid his cheek against her, trying in some small way to give her comfort, but only the truth would begin to mend her pain. "Rin, the truth is not always an easy thing to endure. Once you know it, there's no going back. Are you prepared for that?"

"I'm not prepared for anything anymore, but already I can't go back."

The warmth of her skin. The scent of her. Her fierceness and surprising vulnerability. Everything she was pulled at him. He nuzzled into the silk of her hair and breathed her in one last time. Because after he told her everything, he'd never get close enough to touch her. She'd never allow it.

"Your mother faked her own death."

"Wha...wh...why? Why would she do that? How...could she?"

He sat back on his heels, straddling her. "Your mother—" His phone vibrated in his back pocket. And he knew just who it was. He sighed and answered.

"Goddamnit, Luck!" The husky female voice shouted so loudly Rin's eyes bulged at the sound of the voice. "This isn't the way."

"It's the only way. I'm protecting her. And that means from anything that hurts her, including you. You may have heard, but you don't see what you're doing to her."

"It's not your right. You don't get to choose this life for her," she hollered into his ear.

"No, but your daughter should get the choice."

Luck took the phone from his ear and held it out to Rin.

Chapter Eleven

Her mother. It wasn't possible, but there it was—a sleek black phone being held out to her with a voice on the line so remarkably like her mother's it stung. She reached out a quivering hand. Luck grabbed it, secured her elbow, and lifted her from the floor.

"Stand for just a minute." He stepped to the table and hoisted a chair. But she watched the phone, terrified to lose sight of it, as though this were a dream and any loss of connection with the ground would jar her from sleep. He set the chair behind her and eased her into it like the nurses did for her grandfather. His warm fingers opened her hand, and then he placed the device on her palm.

Rin bit her lips together to keep from crying out. She lifted the phone to her ear and listened. Not even a crackle broke through the other end. "Hello?" she whispered.

"My Rin Bird. Hey, baby." She'd thought she'd forgotten her mother's voice in junior high. She'd smashed in her classroom's windows that day. But now, it was as if she'd heard it only moments ago.

Anger, sadness, elation, and confusion obscured her vision. She'd longed to hear her mother's voice just once more, and now that she did, an unholy rage choked out everything else. Her fist knotted so tightly it shook. Luck's tanned hands bracketed her pale one.

"I know you have so many questions, and that none of this makes sense. I don't blame you for hating me, but I did it all to keep you safe."

"I need answers," she managed.

"And Luck will give them to you. It's not safe for me to speak on the phone."

"I want to see you." Rin said the words even though she knew the response.

"I'd love nothing more, but I can't. Not right now."

"Why not?"

"I haven't been in the States since the day I kissed you goodbye."

"I'll come to you." Desperation pitched her voice to the moon.

"You can't know where I am. Just knowing would get you tortured."

"By who?"

"I have to go, Rin Bird. It made my lifetime just to hear your voice again."

"I love you," Rin croaked.

"I love you, my darling girl."

Chapter Twelve

Luck took the phone from Rin's limp hand. "I've got her."

"Just don't go off and do something stupid like go after Harlow or fall in love with my daughter," Cara said.

He mapped the slight up-turn of Rin's pixie nose. The rose in her thin lips. The strength in the set of her jaw, even after the blows she'd taken today. Out of deference to her mother, he steered clear of the dip of her hips and length of her shapely legs.

"No promises." He hung up and peered at the time—three-oh-four a.m.—then stowed the phone in his pocket.

Rin's eyes glazed as though her brain were shorted out on information overload. Without a word he scooped her into his arms and walked to the bed. As he laid her on the light green sheets he expected a token argument, but got none. She rolled over and buried her face in his pillow. Her light hair splayed in a curtain around her shoulder blades and spilled onto the bed.

He glossed over the buxom swell of her butt, driving his gaze to her sandal-clad feet. One by one he removed her shoes. Her ankles puffed from all her walking. His fingers worked over the swollen skin, rubbing down to her heels and then the arch of her feet.

A tiny red cut flashed like a neon sign at the tender middle of her right foot. "What happened here?" he asked, soothing a wide circle around the tiny wound.

"You." Her voice drifted on a lethargic murmur.

The more he massaged, the further she sank into the mattress. When her breathing evened he tucked her feet beneath the twisted top sheet, straightened it, and raised it to her nape.

Luck raked his hands through his tousled hair. If she thought today was bad, just wait until tomorrow. The hits would just keep on coming. Now he hated it for her, instead of scorning her for her wayward youth. She'd had people in her life who cared about her, and had chosen the street—unlike him. He was grateful she'd taken the rocky path. It prepared her for the truth to come.

Hands in pockets, he shuffled over to the table, tossed the three times rewarmed pizza, flipped the switch on Cara's audio surveillance, and then another for the lights, before shuffling back to the bed by the light of the small corner bathroom. He toed off his riding boots and lost the socks. As much as he disliked sleeping in clothes, he kept the layer between him and Rin because he disliked screaming women more.

Another person sleeping in his space stomped all over the border of strange. It took a handful of minutes before he relaxed enough that his lids hung low. The bed lurched. His eyes shot open. He snapped up and reached for the Sig lying on the old milk crates stacked beside the frame. In the murk he saw no threat. Well, Rin was a threat of a different sort.

He calmed his heart rate, guessing from the restlessness in her jogging legs that she'd been the source of the disturbance. Abandoning the pistol, Luck lay on his side facing the willowy woman and rested his head on his arm. A soft cry broke the silence.

Luck hooked an arm around her middle and tugged her into the spoon of his body so that her back rested against his front. "Rin," he whispered, "it's just a dream."

"No. It's a memory," she sniffled.

"Leave it in the past and sleep."

"I don't know if I can." Her fingers slid between his and held tight.

"Favorite song of all time?"

"What?" she breathed.

"You heard me."

"That's...the hardest question of all time. There are too many great songs. Do you want classic and pop culture? Genre? Subgroup? Because I could give you one for each, but an overall favorite of all time..."

"Quit stalling."

"Fine, but you're not even gonna know the song."

"Give."

"Rap Promoter. A Tribe Called Quest. The Low End Theory."

"You're not dickin' with me are you?"

"I don't have a penis. So, no."

"You're a comedian in the pre-dawn hours, huh?"

"Best. Song. Ever. No-lie." She beat his hand to her chest with each word.

"In that case you have to marry me," he said, only partially kidding.

"Depends on your favorite song," she giggled.

"A Tribe Called Quest. Low End Theory." Her chest stilled except for the beating of her heart. Still he held the suspense.

"Say it," she screeched.

"Excursions."

"I knew it. Damn. That's the best album," she said. "I can't believe you know hip hop."

"I lived it. Best guy my mom ever dated was a music exec. He gave me an old school boom box for my seventh birthday. Nearly busted an eardrum jammin' to Grand Master Flash."

"I'll admit to being jealous. My Walkman wasn't nearly as cool, but I managed some hearing loss anyway." She sighed and nestled his hand between her breasts. "Thank you."

"Try and get some sleep."

She nodded. Luck rested his chin on her silky hair. He drifted in the rhythm of great music and her scent.

"Yes," she breathed.

"Yes?"

"I'll marry you."

"It's a plan then." He smiled and fell asleep with the ridiculous expression on his face. He woke with it there too. And Rin in his arms.

Her dark blue eyes, flecked with shards of green and brown, flitted about his face. Lips pressed into a line that quirked at one side. He'd expected her to flee his embrace the moment her wits returned. From the glint in her expression he could see that they had, but she snuggled into him, wedging a leg between his and clutching the front of his shirt.

Steaming hot lust roused him from morning lethargy. It would just take one move. A simple shift in her direction and she'd let him kiss her. He knew it as well as he knew he shouldn't take advantage of her emotional state. People like them didn't get emotional often, but when they did it heightened every other emotion.

She inhaled to speak.

Luck placed his fingers over her lips. "You need to eat before the questions start. Because once they do, they'll last all day."

She moved the pads of his fingers to her cheek. "I'll eat. Promise. I'm starving. But I want to know a few things first." He scowled, but she continued anyway. "How do you know my mother?"

"She picked me up off the streets of Rio, a bad kid with an even worse attitude."

He waited a second for the pity. But Rin quirked a brow. "You don't have an accent."

He loved her. For understanding and so much more...he loved her. The notion hit him square in the chest. He exhaled against the exquisite pain and held her just a little bit tighter.

"No. My mom followed a boyfriend there, got dumped, and then took up meth to soothe her broken heart. We never made it back to the States."

"Where are you from?"

"Los Angeles. She was going to be a star and now she's dead."

"I'm sorry she wasn't stronger for you."

Damn. Was it him or was the room suddenly blurry? He blinked furiously and ground his teeth. What a perfect thing to say.

"So, you spent time with my mom?"

"Yeah," he said, thankful for the change of topic. "But not the mom you know. She's former CIA. She took me under her wing, drove me into the ground, broke me, and then built me back. Taught me to do... everything from living the straight and narrow to building a bomb out of stuff you have in your kitchen. She gave me a future that didn't include jacking cars or a body bag."

Rin's eyes pinched shut. "CIA?"

"One of the best."

Her long lashes rested on her cheeks so long he began to think she'd passed out from the shock. Finally they fluttered opened. "Seems pretty dangerous, what you do."

"When you have the training it's not near as dangerous as the stuff we did on the streets."

"Truth." She grimaced.

"As payment, I watched over you."

"For how long?"

"A little more than a year."

She puffed out her lips. "And I never knew. I was never meant to know."

"You weren't," he admitted.

She broke eye contact and buried her face under his chin for several minutes. He enjoyed the feel of her against him, the unexpected comfort.

"Let's eat," she whispered. "I can't stomach any more right now."

Chapter Thirteen

Rin stepped from the narrow shower stall, dried with a towel that smelled of Luck, and then riffled through her bag for something to wear. She walked from the tiny room with a pair of cutoffs and a loose vintage tank with the MTV logo. Luck had traded his T-shirt for one that looked like it had seen battle several times and a pair of jeans to match. He set two glasses on the table on either side of a tray of steaming pizza.

"Sorry, I didn't expect company and I haven't been to the grocery in a few days."

"Cereal wouldn't cut it this morning anyway." She sat opposite him and took a long pull on her milk. "You know, it should freak me out way more than it does that you've watched me for a year." The damp ends of her hair tickled her chest. She swatted it back. "I mean, you probably heard me burp when I was home alone."

"It was cute." He bit into his pizza and waggled his brows.

"Burps aren't cute."

"They are when they come out of something so tiny."

"Ew."

"It's natural." He shrugged.

Rin scowled at him over the remaining pie. After several minutes in silent stalemate Luck reached for another slice and they finished the leftovers in record time. Rin collapsed back in her chair, completely full and still not ready to tackle the drama sure to come. Ready or not, her mind mulled over the scarce facts.

"She's proud of you." Luck dropped the bomb while snagging her napkin and empty glass. He turned away to clean the cups and she was glad for the reprieve.

How could her mother be proud? "I was a mess."

"She understood why. Besides, you turned it around on your own. No one did that for you."

"I had help."

"Everyone needs it at some point. Some just aren't smart enough to realize it. You were." He placed the glasses on a dishtowel and sauntered his loose hips her way. "You turning your life around is what got this ball rolling in the first place. She never expected you to apply for a government job. When you took your position with the DOD it flagged the CIA. They put a team in place to watch you. Nate. Zach. Jen."

"What about Gregory?" Her heart clenched, while she prayed her friend wasn't in league with the enemy. They had been friends before her big girl job. No, that wasn't accurate. She'd met him while shopping for career clothes at the boutique where Gregory used to work before he'd passed the bar exam. Her hopes dove.

"I'm sorry." He shoved his hands in his pockets and shook his head. "They wanted to know if your mother had contacted you. They always suspected she'd faked her death, but could never find her."

Rin's stomach popped up road blocks and hoisted its strike signs. It grumbled and roared.

Somehow she swallowed past the rising acid. Maybe her voice would work.

"Is she a bad guy?"

"In the eyes of the US government, she's a traitor. But there's always more to the story." He offered his hand. "We need some fresh air."

When they made it to the other side of the big-ass door, Luck headed up the steps instead of down. She used the railing and his hand for support, but by the third flight she limped from the bruise Nate had left on her back and the ache in her calves.

"Up you go," he said, squatting low on the steps and presenting her with his back. She just stared at the fine V of his defined lats visible from the cut of his shirt. "You can hop on my back or I'll toss you over my shoulder. Your choice."

She hopped onto his back, cinched her legs around his middle, and hugged his lean muscles. As he walked, his soft hair tickled the side of her face. Luck between her thighs fooled with her brain. They reached the roof access and he pushed through the door.

The clear blue sky opened up as far as she could see. In the distance skyscrapers and monuments dotted the horizon, but the other buildings that surrounded them hunched smaller than this one. He stooped, released his grip on her thighs, and she slid down his back. The friction curled her toes. She channeled her angst over the unfolding drama to calm her aching core.

They fell in step together, heading for a patio table with a throw-back boombox on top and an umbrella fanning out from a hole in its middle.

"Not scared you're going to get sniped?"

He put a finger over his mouth. She shut hers and moved closer to him. Gravel crunched under their feet. The sun beat on their skin. By the time they reached the table no bullets had taken them out. Luck pressed a button on the radio and a DJ for WKYS announced Iggy Azalea's Black Widow as the next on tap.

"If they knew we were here they'd come in hot. Try and take us alive," he shrugged.

"Jesus! Give me the quick and dirty version. I need to understand this."

Luck pulled out a chair and offered her the shade of the umbrella. She sat. He took the chair next to her and stretched out his legs.

"Your mom was recruited out of college by the CIA. She worked Russia, bringing in pivotal intel that helped propel the end of the Cold War. The man she used as her mark—your father—was the Soviet Minister of Defense. Years later he tracked your mother back to the States. She covered her tracks well and it took him a long time, but when you were a girl he showed up at your house, tried to take you back to Russia with him as payment for her betrayal."

"That's why she killed him?"

"Yep."

A wave of nausea crashed over her, suffocating her in the heat of the day. Rin stood and hurried to the edge of the roof. Luck's footsteps sounded right behind her. The tar-topped building lip burned her palms, but she didn't much care. She leaned over and sucked a breath, then another. Luck's hand slipped inside the waistband of her shorts and clamped down.

"I'm not going to jump."

"Maybe I just want to cop a feel."

"You already did that in the morgue."

"It was nice," his sexy voice rumbled.

A flash of heat that had nothing to do with the rays of the sun warmed her skin. Rin hung her head between her shoulders and watched the tiny cars roll by. "I don't understand any of this."

"You may never."

"Why toss herself off a building in front of me?"

"You weren't supposed to be there, but your babysitter got sick. Your grandfather brought you to the party. She didn't know until after... that you saw."

"Why fake her death in the first place, if she killed him?"

"Because she killed him. Ansya Popov, his lead spy, would never have stopped looking for her. And she would have found you."

"Why is my mother an enemy of the State?"

"In an effort to flush her out, Popov forged evidence that Cara, your mom, sold secrets while behind the curtain. She figured it would be twice as hard for her to stay hidden with two groups looking for her."

Rin fished her lips and thought. "Okay, after all this time why would Popov continue looking for her? Why does any of it matter anymore?"

"Now it's more about principal for her. She has no country. No place to call home and she wanted that for your mother. Also, Popov and your father were rumored to have been lovers before she was taken captive by the North Koreans."

A cold sweat broke out over Rin's skin. "Oh my God, she's here. Nate talked to her the other day."

"Here, in the States?" he asked, whirling her around to face him.

"Here in DC. The tape! The tape you stole, where is it?"

Chapter Fourteen

Luck sprinted down two flights before he remembered Rin's legs hurt. He turned to check on her, but she blew past him. Adrenaline was an amazing thing. They went round, stampeding down side by side until they reached his loft. He tugged the keys from his pocket and popped the lock on the chest at the foot of his bed.

"Holy shit. Is it legal to have all those guns?" Rin panted over his shoulder.

"It's legal to have that many, but not all the types. And the RPG is a big no-no."

"Awesome."

He chuckled and grabbed the mini tape he'd confiscated from her the day before. "Didn't have time to listen to it yesterday. I had to get to your place. I knew you wouldn't stay with Nate. At least, I hoped you wouldn't, even though it would have been safer for you."

"Why'd you hope—"

He depressed play on the device he'd bought after he figured out Nate used them to record her, deliberately ignoring her question. He really shouldn't go there. He fast-forwarded through their morning routine and again through the silence after. When the tape played again a female voice berated Nate for the meeting location.

Yep, it had been a bad idea on the guy's part. The conversation went on. The evidence mounted that this woman was in fact Ansya Popov. The clincher came at the end, just like Rin had said it would. Euphoria lightened the heavy weight on his shoulders.

Before he could stop himself, he wrapped his hand around Rin's nape and sealed his mouth over hers. She tasted even better than she smelled. Pizza mixed with a delicate vanilla to drive him mad, and he didn't even use tongue.

Luck eased back, dug his fingers into her hair, repositioned her, and went back for more. This time he teased her upper lip until she opened for him. He suctioned his mouth to her lower lip and nibbled before delving his tongue inside.

Her impatient mouth moved to accommodate him, becoming a pliant form of the woman he'd yet to fully discover. And Lord, how he wanted to discover every part, every nuance.

A *bang* forced him back. He reached for his gun before he realized the noise was from the tape.

"I fell," she explained in a dreamy voice.

Me too.

His hand slipped from her hair and caressed her lips. "When I have time, I'd like to kiss you for an entire day."

"And it can't be today?" she asked on a sigh.

"It's almost half over."

"You could make up for those hours tomorrow."

Luck brushed his knuckles over her cheek and leaned in, brushing their lips with measured ease. "I need to make a phone call."

Chapter Fifteen

Luck stuffed his free hand in his pocket and Rin hoped it was because he couldn't keep his hand off her otherwise. She wanted to strip his clothes off with her teeth and lick every inch of the muscled skin she'd seen far too little of. He'd enticed her the moment his decadent voice had rumbled in her ear and every moment since. Even when she wanted to sock him on the chin, another part yearned to pull him close and never turn him loose.

He speed-dialed her mother on speakerphone. She could seduce him while he was on the phone. But, she wanted this to be special. No, this was special.

He was different than anyone she'd ever been with. He was so much like her, walled off from the rest of the world. She'd never let anyone close, and somehow he fit next to her most intimate thoughts and hidden emotions. And she liked him there.

"Luck?" her mother's raspy voice carried an anxious tone over the line.

"We're good here. Better than. Your daughter is a damn genius. She found Popov." A smile curved one side of his reddened mouth.

"How?" Cara Lee snapped like no ghost she'd ever heard.

"A conversation she overheard between Popov and Harlow yesterday in person in her condo," Luck explained.

"How did that happen without you knowing?" she growled.

"Don't yell at him." Rin snapped the words with a force that silenced them all for a pile of seconds. Luck's gaze narrowed, but amusement clung in his crooked grin. "He had no way to know I'd seen a text to Nate that made me suspicious enough to snoop after I should have left for work. Besides, I'm not his burden. I'm my own responsibility."

His quiet delight vanished with his smile. "That's not your call, Rin."

"Mom, tell him I'm not his mission anymore," Rin demanded.

"It's not her call either," Luck whispered. "I'm not protecting you for her."

"Then who the hell are you doing it for?" her mother hollered.

"Me," he said. "I'm protecting her because I want her...safe, cared for."

Rin looked at her feet in total shock at the conviction in his timbre. Her grandparents had protected her as much as they could. They were family. They tried to make up for the absence of her mother. What did he have to gain from protecting her?

As if he'd heard her thoughts, his pointing finger pressed over her heart. He held it there until finally she met his gaze. Luck cupped her cheek. So much emotion channeled through his intense gaze and that simple touch. Rin molded her hand over his and held him close.

"I'll take care of Popov," her mother said. "You two stay put. Do you hear me?"

"Yes." Luck's thumb hovered over the end button.

"Damien Luck," Cara Lee scolded, "you remember what I said to you."

"Yep. You remember I said no promises." With those words he ended the call. He tossed the phone into the open trunk and cradled her other cheek in his hand.

She noticed the lightest sprinkling of freckles across the bridge of his nose. Those tiny dots twisted her durable heart like a clown balloon, changing the unfeeling organ into a squeaking, fragile piece of plastic he could crush under his boot. And though she'd honed the instinct to run at the first hint of such a liability, she tilted her chin and lost herself in his clear eyes.

"No one has ever stood up for me." The small creases on his lips bunched. His jaw worked and he swallowed as though struggling for composure. "I haven't needed it for a long time, but you..." His grip urged her forward. "You make me want things I've never needed. You make me weak and strong at the same time."

His mouth lowered and brushed her cheek with tender reverence. Those soft lips kissed her chin, her brow, her nose, as though she were fragile. In his arms she was and at the same time, she was powerful too—just like he'd said.

The emotion had her shifting, dancing uncomfortably in her shoes. He released his hold and stepped back, a pained expression drawing his beautiful face.

"What didn't you promise her?" Rin asked.

"You don't really want to know the answer to that question," he warned.

"Try me."

He stood, broad chest only inches from hers, and smirked. His taste still lingered on her lips and he mocked her.

"I'm not a child," she goaded. "You can't be any older than me."

"Street wise, I'm forty, shorty."

"And real world?"

"You've got me by a year, old lady."

"So, give," she ordered.

"Fine. She warned me not to go after Nate and not to fall in love with you."

The first part she could see, but the second jerked the rug out from under her feet. Rin clamped her mouth together to keep from sputtering until she formulated a response. She almost took a step back, but refused to be cowed by the arrogant pout of his lips.

"Why would you go after Nate?"

"Let's just say he's not my favorite guy."

"Why not? He's not really the bad guy here."

"You're kidding me, right?"

His jaw set. He folded his arms and the bulge of his biceps swelled.

"He doesn't know Popov is a Soviet spy."

"He tried to beat the shit out of you to maintain his cover. A man who can screw a woman one night and smack her around the next..." His teeth flashed. "...is worse than Popov. At least she's loyal."

Rin gasped and her heart cramped. "You heard everything. That's what you were saying last night."

"Just stop." His teeth ground together. "I'm a dick. I shouldn't have said anything."

Her stomach pitched. He probably watched her and Nate go at it all the time. She bristled. "I'm not going to apologize for liking sex."

He scoffed. "You shouldn't and I didn't ask you to."

"But you have this judgmental look that's making me sick to my stomach."

"Well, talking about it isn't great for me either," he snapped.

"What? Are you a prude?" She folded her arms across her breasts, shoving what little cleavage she possessed into his face.

"Just let it go or you'll end up pissed," he said, lifting his palm from his arm.

"I'm already pissed." Her cheeks burned.

"You deserve to be loved, to have a guy love your body, to worship it with everything he has. He used you like a fist for a quick jerk, and then he rolled over and went to sleep."

"Did you ever think that I was the one using him? No, you didn't, because society has programmed you to think that way. A woman should find a nice guy, fall in love, get married, and have some snotty little kids. Well, I don't do mushy. I don't do love."

"You never let anyone get close," he said with a sad shake of his head. "Me neither. But I'm willing to admit that holding the world at a distance sucks. It's exhausting and damn lonely."

"Screw you," she yelled because his words hit too close to her version of the truth, the one she couldn't admit to herself.

"Not just for pleasure." His thick brow arched.

"For what, then?"

"Your heart."

"I don't have one."

"I saw it last night."

"You must have been deliriously tired."

"No, you were. That's how I caught a glimpse." He leaned forward, snatched his phone from the chest, and then closed and locked it. His lips opened to say more, but he hesitated. His heels caught traction as he turned and headed for the door.

"Where are you going?" she yelled at the back of his head.

"Out."

"She said to stay put."

"She also said not to fall in love with you."

"That shouldn't be too hard," she quipped.

"Too fucking late is what it is." He reached the door, turned, and heaved the screeching metal, rolling it between them.

"You can't love me," she panted against the quivering of her heart. "You don't know me."

"I watched you for a year, Rin. I know you better than you know yourself. Being at that bus stop wasn't an accident. Making a connection with you was, as far as the mission went, but for me that was it. You were it. " Their gazes locked. The eroded metal door Luck closed slowly broke the trance.

The clank of the latch into place triggered the explosion in her heart and mind.

Chapter Sixteen

He came back three hours later to find her asleep on the bed. Her tear-stained face snuggled into his pillow. Guilt for leaving her gnawed, but if he'd stayed they'd have accomplished nothing but hurting each other. He unpacked and stowed the groceries before slicing up potatoes, seasoning them, and forming hamburger patties.

"Where are you going now," she whispered from across the room as he headed to the door.

When he turned she shoved the hair back from her face and wiped at her eyes. "There's a grill on the roof." He presented the tray of food and utensils in his hand as explanation. "If you can stand my company, you're welcome to come."

She rested her head on her knees. "You left. Not me."

"Would you have, if you could've?"

"Probably. It's what people like us do."

He nodded, hating the truth of it.

"Let me pee and I'll go with you."

After she finished her business they fell into step on the long walk to the roof.

"Ever think of installing an elevator?"

"There's a lift."

"Then why are we hauling our asses up the steps?"

"It's good for the ticker."

"In that case you'll live forever."

He held the door for her at the top. Rin sat at the patio table and stared off into the sky while he heated the charcoal and cooked. "There's beer and water in the mini fridge to the left of the door, if you want something."

Her gaze catalogued him for a full minute. "Have you ever been in love?"

"When you're scraping to stay alive there's no room for love."

"And now?"

"I'm not scraping. I have a trade—if you will— and it pays well enough that I only contract out a few times a year."

"And love?"

He flipped the burgers. "To be in love, the object of your love has to reciprocate those feelings. And she's not ready for that."

Her footsteps crunched the gravel as she shuffled to the fridge and then to his side. She handed over a beer with the top already twisted off. "Can I help?"

"You just did." His lips rimmed the cold bottle and he took a long pull. "Why'd you choose the street? You had a choice."

"You didn't."

"That's life."

"I was angry at the world. So, I channeled my rage the only way I knew how."

"I bet they never saw you coming. I sure didn't."

He glimpsed the smile she hid behind her bottle.

They watched the sun slip beneath the horizon and ate in easy silence. He took the remaining six buns, loaded them with lettuce, tomato, and condiments, and then topped them with a patty each.

Her eyes bugged at the remaining food. "You planning to eat burgers for a week?"

"Nope." He handed her a stack of napkins. "Will you wrap these while I clean up?"

"Sure," she grinned with wary eyes.

After everything was situated he hauled the large tray and they headed down. The closer they came to his flat the higher unease crept up his neck. Rin be-bopped through the open doorway. He lagged.

"What is it?" she asked, spinning on her heels.

"I have to do something. I'll be right back." He hurried down the stairs before she could respond.

At the back door, Luck punched in his security code and the lock popped. He twisted the knob and stepped into the alley.

"Smells like our lucky day," Ottis's thick voice rumbled. The big man's white teeth peeked from behind his thin lips and he offered his hand. He wore long sleeves and pants despite the heat. Alley grime dirtied his boots.

Luck returned the veteran's sturdy grip. "Burgers and all the trimmings."

"Ooh-we. Me and the boys'll sleep good tonight," Ottis said, patting his slim belly.

"I hope so." Luck offered Ottis the tray.

"I thank you, mister. Sure wish you'd tell me your name. You've been feeding us for months now and it's hard praying for someone who hasn't got a name."

"You keep up with those prayers, Ottis. I can use all I can get."

"Naw, you're all right with the Lord. He told me so." Ottis saluted and walked off to divide out the food amongst his friends.

Luck locked the door back and headed for the stairs, but stopped mid-room. Rin propped a hip on the Bentley. "What about your tray?"

"He'll bring it back tomorrow morning."

"You lied to me, Damien Luck." She crossed her arms and canted her head.

"I've never lied to you."

"You've never meant to lie to me, but you're lying to yourself too. So, I won't hold it against you."

Luck plowed a hand through his hair.

"You told me you weren't a good guy. Apparently I'm not the only one here who doesn't know themselves."

Chapter Seventeen

He crossed the room, grabbed her hand from the crook of her arm, and gave a gentle tug, coaxing her toward the apartment. The way he gnawed on his cheek endeared him to her all the more. His generosity made him uncomfortable.

"It didn't escape my notice yesterday, but I had plenty of other things to hammer out first. What are you doing with a Bentley?"

"I needed it for the job. No one questions a Bentley rolling through downtown DC—or the person in it. Other times I need to be invisible. Others, maneuverable. It's just a tool."

"It's a fine piece of machine," she corrected.

He stopped tugging her up the steps and turned. "It's a future for Ottis. When your mom is done with me, I'll sell it, buy a food truck, and he'll run it for me."

"Like I said," she placed a hand over his heart, "you lied."

His brows fell, shadowing his eyes. "Can the good we do make up for the bad in our past?"

"I surc hopc so."

He folded his hand around hers and urged her up the steps. Inside, he shoved the door in place, turned, and framed her face in his hands. His gentle pull drew her in. Luck licked at her mouth, stoking a fire that had been banking and building heat so overwhelming it might char them both. The purity of his affection seized her while his lips captured.

"Rin, let me love you," he said against her mouth.

There was that word. He'd already wormed his way into her heart, but that word rattled every ghost in her collection. "I'm scared."

"Me too, but I won't let it stop me. Only you can do that."

"This is crazy. What do we know about each other?"

"The important things. The rest will come, if you let it, if you trust me and yourself enough to find out." His playful smile returned. "I mean, you did already agree to marry me."

His callused thumb traced her grin, the roughened pad scraping her surprisingly sensitive flesh. "Guess I need to know if you can bone before we make it official." She shrugged.

"You're crazy," he laughed. "But this isn't about a good screw. It's about connecting."

His forehead rested on hers as it had when he pinned her to the floor. A forest of long lashes rimmed the eyes that saw every blemish on her soul and accepted them as a part of her. Eyes that allowed her to peer inside to his scarred depths.

Rin's hands coasted over his rock hard shoulders. She crushed his threadbare T-shirt in her palms and pulled him closer still. "Make love to me, Luck."

He enveloped her in his arms. Her feet dangled above the ground. The crushing weight of his embrace secured her to his body. Pounding heart to pounding heart. Light scruff rasped her chin. She closed her eyes and felt him. His lips molded to her greedy mouth with a sensuousness that made the world disappear, taking all her problems with it.

Slow, steady strokes toyed with her tongue. She waited for his big move to get her flat on her back, but it didn't come. Impatience curled in her belly, peaking her nipples. The longer he exalted her mouth the higher her anxiety ratcheted, distorting her need. Panic—the feeling of being stripped to the soul—incited her.

Rin wrapped her legs around his hips. Her hips rolled up and down the length of his full shaft. A moan seeped from her throat. Control soothed her. It abated her uncertainty.

When he took a step toward the bed, and then another, she sucked his tongue into the back of her throat, giving a taste of what she could do with his cock, given the chance. Instead of tossing her onto the bed and covering her with his eager body, he turned away from it, sat on the edge, and pulled back. She clenched her eyes, too scared of what she might see.

"You're the bravest, strongest person I've ever met, Rin. Don't let fear lead you in this. You'll fleece us both." His arms loosened around her, smoothed up her back, over her shoulders, down her breast, across the globes of her ass, around her legs. He gentled her. "I'll fuck you so hard and fast you'll scream for mercy. But this time, I won't be rushed." He yanked her mouth to his and began the gentle persuasion all over again. "If you feel bared and angsty, look at me. I feel it too, but I refuse to run from it."

She opened her eyes and found his blues staring back at her. "How can you open your eyes and kiss?"

"I don't, not usually, but I want to see you."

Little by little, Rin eased her grip on his shirt and her ever-present control. She relaxed into his kiss. Fell into his blurry gaze. Traced the features of his face with her fingers.

The room shifted beneath her feet again. Instinct to seize control frazzled her nerves. "Love me, Rin." Luck's smooth voice croaked the words. The emotion layering his voice sucked her under and diluted her panic.

"I am loving you," she whispered. She took control. Not for her, but for him. A warmth she'd never experienced heated her lips over his skin, as if something deeper than the physical attraction connected them. "I have been since that stupid bus stop."

With unhurried fingers Rin gripped his shirt and inched it over his head. Where she expected smooth skin, ragged scars littered his sharply muscled torso. Their gazes met. Rin exhaled and pulled her tank top over her head. She swept her finger over her initiation burns, then glided her other hand over the rippled flesh covering his ribs.

He had other discolorations. An old slicing wound bisected his right pectoral. A round scar too large to be a cigarette burn bloomed over his abdomen. She traced each mark and each unblemished swath of his beautiful skin, while his hands mirrored the action on her body. They both knew the struggle of life on the street and the battles of life on the straight and narrow, which were sometimes greater because civilization had rules.

His thumb padded her nipple. Rin forgot their past strife and arched into his touch, thankful for once that with her little breasts she didn't have to wear a bra. Her head fell back. The wet heat of his mouth tugged on her engorged flesh. Sensation mimicked each pull in her throbbing clit. She tried to dampen her reaction, but she writhed, desperate for more.

Luck rolled her onto the bed and levered over her body. He yanked her shorts off her hips without unfastening them. The muscles in his arms and back bunched into corded lines as he worked. His heavy weight settled between her thighs.

She watched in slack-jawed amazement while, one by one, he kissed every ugly scar across her belly until his lips crested her mons. His wicked eyes locked with hers a moment before he shoved her thighs over his shoulders. Luck licked his lips and then stroked the wet pillows over her aching nub.

Their fingers intertwined over her hip. Rin held on for dear life as he kissed between her legs. She'd been eaten out, sucked, lashed, but never kissed. His shoulders opened her farther and his lips tormented with measured pace and pressure. Her head lolled side to side.

A slide of his tongue through her folds shot pleasure to every extremity. Her hands squeezed his in a silent plea. His gaze lifted. The slickness of her desire coated his mouth. Eyes locked on hers, he flattened his tongue and laved her clit.

The sight of him hungry and sating himself at her altar topped her list on eroticism. She curled at the sight, her shoulder blades bowing off the bed. His hands shifted from beneath hers, rounded her bottom, and did wicked things to her distended flesh she couldn't follow for the bliss they poured onto her.

Finally she figured it out. One finger toyed with her aching rosette, while another massaged her from inside, while another imprisoned her clitoris. All the while his tongue bathed her back to front.

Oh God, yes.

She exploded, shot into the universe in so many directions she'd never find all her pieces. A quiet whimper of overwhelming delight echoed with his rasped breaths. He scattered her. He made her look deeper, past the hurt and fear, to... possibilities.

Luck withdrew his fingers and kissed a trail over her blemished stomach. His blond hair curled at the base of his scalp, where sweat beaded. The flat of his tongue danced over her navel and up to her breasts. He bathed each mound with care and attention, driving moisture to her already soaked folds. His shoulders raised over her like lean-cut granite.

He pinched her erect buds between his thumb and forefinger. A moan slipped from her lips. She shimmied beneath him. An unabashed smile arched his lips.

"Enjoying this are you?" she whispered.

"Mmm." His teeth nipped her collarbone, running a trail to her neck and up to her chin. "I'm enjoying you."

Rin grinned like a fiend.

He yanked her thighs to meet his swollen cock, held captive by his jeans. His zipper sang and his knuckles brushed her clit.

She framed his face and assaulted him with her tongue. "Love me, Luck."

"I do." His blues held hers as he stroked her with the bare head of his penis. "I already do." His wide crown breached her body. They both gasped.

Rin dug her hands into his soft locks and held him as tightly as her strength would allow. He didn't withdraw, only shoved deeper, and deeper still, until at last they were connected more than the act, more than the words. They just were. Despite the situation. Despite the ridiculous swiftness. Despite their pasts.

Luck gathered her in his arms and caressed her from inside out with long, even drives. He filled her to the point of pain that melted into inexplicable pleasure. His head brushed the tender spot so easily it rushed a climax she wasn't prepared for.

Her breaths grew short then stilled altogether. He rode her through the ecstasy that crumbled her soul and immediately built it up better than it had ever been. He leaned back, spread his jean-clad knees wide, and rested on his heels. His hands latched onto the top of her hips. As he lifted her bottom, screwing his length in and out of her, the plateaus of his pecs and abdomen bunched and flexed.

"Are you on the pill?"

"Yes."

"May I come inside you?"

No one had ever asked her that before and no one had ever done it bare. The thought spurred her excitement. "Yes," she panted.

He arched into her, rubbing the hard V of his muscled groin onto her clit. His hands massaged her cheeks with each pump. Rin cupped her breast and rocked with his rhythm.

His tempo ramped and the careful constraints he'd imposed on himself slipped. The bite of his fingers clawed at her flesh. The laser focus of his gaze faltered. His eyes slammed shut. The veins in his neck bulged. His head craned toward the sky. And Rin loved every deviant moment.

He shouted his climax to the world. His hot spurts and brazen exhibition of masculinity hastened her to long, heavy moans. She convulsed around him and drifted in euphoria. He gathered her into his arms. The world tilted. Her joyous state stayed firmly entrenched—and probably would stay, no matter where she went. As long as Luck was there to help her face her demons.

Her head nested in the crook of his neck. The *thud* of his heartbeat pounded in her ear. He caressed her back and held her close.

The words tiptoed over her lips, but she just wasn't ready to admit to him what she felt. Though, how had her actions not shown him? She timed her breaths with his as much as she could, relaxed, and enjoyed the feel of him still firmly embedded in her body.

Rin woke to easy strokes and kisses feathered over her face. On top this time, she took the lead, sitting up, and smiled down at Luck's sleepy face. They'd obviously both fallen asleep after the first round, leaving the lights burning bright. She lifted his hands from her thighs and pressed them against her breasts.

Bracing hers on his firm chest, mirroring her action, she rode him with a gentle undulation of her hips. He thickened to brimming. The scrape of his fingers toyed over her tender flesh.

"You're so beautiful. All of you," he whispered.

She rocked harder, unable to say how much she needed him, but desperate to show him. But she worked herself into an orgasm too quickly. She arched wildly and came, slicking his cock with her cream.

Luck rolled her onto her back, flipped her, and wrenched one leg high. He seated himself to the hilt, pillowing against the softness of her bottom. His arms held her and his hips thrust with a desperation she'd not yet seen in him. He licked at her nape. One of his hands slid between her and the bed.

He collected their juices from his shaft and then coated her clit. His finger strummed her to the brink as he pumped himself there, pounding in and out of her with abandon.

"Come with me, Rin."

She fell with him into a heart-stopping orgasm. Luck tensed and came panting in her hair. He kissed her from shoulder to nape as he came down from the ultimate high. He spooned her like he had the first night and sleep reclaimed her.

A piercing alarm jolted her from sleep.

Not the wake-up call she'd looked forward to.

Luck launched from the bed, a large pistol strangled by his hand. With the other he tossed her clothes onto the bed. "They're here. Get dressed."

"Who?"

"Popov."

She shoved through the head of her tank and lurched her long legs into the holes of her shorts, foregoing panties. "How do you know it isn't some common thug, like you or me six years ago?"

"I set a triple catch alarm. Only someone highly trained would think to look for a double, and even fewer know how to override it."

Luck snapped the button on his pants, pushed a button on the cell, and yanked on his shirt. He shoved his feet into his boots. "Come on," he urged, holding out his hand.

This time she grabbed it without pause. He pulled her up and boosted her toward the bathroom. She ran to it, but stopped at the door, waiting for him.

"Get in and stay put." He dropped to his knees in front of the chest. The lock gave way and he shoved the lid high. "Go, Rin."

"Not without you."

Luck grumbled, strapping on a bulky vest with guns and ammo that bulged the pockets. Gun still in hand, he shut the lid without a sound. He consumed the distance between them in two strides. His hand planted over her heart and pushed her back. "So help me, Rin," his voice thickened, "if you don't stay here and do as I ask... if you don't trust me to protect you." His Adam's apple quaked and the lightness in his eyes clouded over. "If something happens to you... I'll regret every day of my life until they toss the dirt on my body."

"I trust you."

He drew a breath. "In the corner. Get low and stay there as long as it takes."

Her head bobbed and tears distorted what could be her last moment with the first and last man she'd ever love.

"Go." He disappeared from the doorway.

Rin shrank into the corner. Hot moisture rained onto her cheeks. She buried her face against her knees. A deep breath filled her lungs. She focused and reached for the steely resolve she'd relied on for so long.

About the time she found it two whispered shots knifed the silence. Rin balled her fists. She clung desperately to the promise she made. Luck's determination to love her and the faith she had in his ability to protect her soothed the nerves jittering her entire body.

The unmistakable screech of the metal door ricocheted off the walls in the flat. A loud thwack followed. The sickening sounds she'd heard at her condo when Nate and Luck fought resumed, but abruptly died.

"I thought you were out of the country. I could have killed you," Luck barked.

"I trained you better than that," Cara Lee's voice rasped.

Rin's stomach swan dived off a cliff and refused to surface. She covered her mouth to keep the agonizing screech of joy and misery from escaping.

"Are you hurt?" Luck asked.

"Just a scratch. Popov always did like the blade. I don't guess she likes it much now, though," her mom said.

"You drew her out. You used Rin as bait?" Luck yelled.

"Yes."

"Are you out of your damn mind? You put her in danger."

"No, I didn't. She had you."

"And what if something had happened to you?" he demanded.

"Again I say, she has you. I get the feeling you're better for her than I am."

"Nothing can compare to the love of a mother. Nothing."

"Where is she?" the familiar and hardly recognizable voice whispered.

"Where is Popov and where are her men?"

"My team has the agents. The Potomac will get Popov. I didn't move on my own."

"Who'd you use?"

"Mercs."

Footsteps sounded across the floor and she knew he walked loudly to give her a moment to prepare for their arrival. They paused halfway and

Velcro screeched. Then he was there, crouching in front of her.

"I'm sorry," he breathed, reaching out a hand to steady hers.

"Why are you sorry?" she breathed.

"I'm sorry you're in here terrified when you didn't have to be. I'm sorry I'll hate your mother for a long time for putting you in danger. And I'm a little sorry it's over, because now you don't need me." He kissed her hand and helped her to her feet. "Are you ready to see your mom?"

She clung to his side and nodded. He walked her out like a personal crutch. It was the only way her legs would function.

When she rounded the corner her vision narrowed to an older version of herself. Her mother's hair flattened to her head in a sleek ponytail. The tiniest wrinkles gathered at the corners of her crystal blue eyes.

Rin smiled past the tears and torment. There would be time for questions and rage later. Right now, her mother had returned from the dead.

Cara Lee covered her mouth on a quiet sob. "I'm so sorry, my baby." Tears flooded her eyes.

Rin held tight to Luck's hand, but walked forward until she was toe-to-toe with her mother. "I've missed you."

The arms that had cradled her from the day of her birth to the day of her mother's death wrapped Rin in warmth. Luck released her hand. She squeezed her mother and they sobbed together. For the time they'd missed. For the time they had to come. Rin cried and laughed.

Finally she gripped that mettle she'd forged long ago and straightened. She cradled her mom's cut cheek and reached for Luck. And his hand was right where she'd left it. He enveloped her hand in his own and she tugged him forward.

"Mom, I'd like you to meet my fiancé, Damien Luck."

Her mom's sandy brown brows shot toward the sky. Behind her Luck coughed on a gasp. She turned and hit him with a soft glare. "You said I had to marry you. There's no backing out now."

Suddenly Rin dangled above the ground. Luck hugged her to his chest and kissed her full on the lips.

"I love you," she whispered in his ear.

"So, I guess I passed your bone test," he whispered back.

"Oh yeah," she giggled, more at peace than she'd ever been.

Chapter Eighteen

A deep masculine cough rolled across the room like a thunderhead.

Before Rin registered fear or surprise, Luck jerked her to his side. His shoulder and torso shielded her, while his other arm snapped up a pistol. Her mother beat him to the punch.

Cara Lee's barrel centered the Kevlar-vested chest of a man that gobbled up the open doorway. Her mother's gun lifted to his easy smile. For a split second, Rin thought he was one of the mercenaries her mother had hired. But then, why would she hold a line on him so sure the veins in her elegant neck bulged and the faint lines at the corner of her eyes thinned in concentration?

Apart from the man's strapping build, the battle equipment hanging from every conceivable pocket and hook on his vest, and his calculating gaze, he didn't seem ready to fight.

"I sure didn't mean to break up a moment." The stranger offered his palms and rolled his hips, shifting his weight to one side. His accent practically painted on cowboy boots, jeans, and a big brass buckle.

"Move on and you may live to regret it." Luck's grip tightened on her back.

"I'm not here to cause trouble," the man drawled.

"From my point of view, you're nothing but trouble." Cara raked her gaze over his battle clad body.

"Cara Lee," the man's thick Texas rumble poured her name like syrup. "More than most, you should know... looks can be deceiving."

Her mother swallowed and her ribs pressed against the fabric of her fitted black shirt.

"I'd like y'all to come with me." The man lowered one hand to his side and extended the other to her mother.

"No." Her mother side stepped, placing herself in front of Rin and Luck.

A small red dot danced across Luck's shoulder. Rin's throat clogged, but two words wheezed between her lips. "Please, no."

Her heart dropped onto the floor as the dots multiplied over her mother's and lover's heads and chests.

VIRTUES
A BASE BRANCH NOVELLA

Once they're gone, can you ever get them back?

As a CIA spy turned traitor to her country, Cara Lee kissed her virtues goodbye long ago. After seventeen years, her retribution ended with the burial of her enemy and a fresh start with her daughter. If only she could forgive herself enough to rebuild their relationship.

Luck—her daughter's fiancé—wasn't Cara's only attempt at atonement. She took Marina Sorensen off a Swedish street corner and schooled her in the art of survival. Too bad the girl sold her and Luck out to the thugs of Brödraskapet.

Her disciplined nature prods Cara to tie the loose end—one way or the other. But the commander of the UN's special forces has other plans. The last thing she wants is another government job. Given an ultimatum—and a babysitter—she plays along.

Tyler Grace should have been a farmer in east Texas, but the universe had other plans. A tactical expert for the Base Branch, when he finds a problem, he seeks the best way to fix it. Cara presents an obstacle he's ill prepared to conquer—but he'll die trying.

Struggling to sort through her past, Cara clings to the one virtue she has left, while Tyler dares to prove she never lost them.

VARIATIONS
A BASE BRANCH NOVEL

Decisions split paths. Bad decisions compound and suddenly you are no more than variations of yourself.

Marina Sorensen rots in a prison of her own making. The bars are the thick arms and meaty hands of Brödraskapet thugs who make money selling her body. Her guilt is the unbreakable shackle. Loneliness is her ever tightening noose. Trading her life for the survival of another is her only salvation.

For Base Branch operative Oliver Knight an eliminate and rescue mission in hostile territory against a brotherhood of brutal sons-of-bitches is another adventure. Downtime between missions in foreign locales with exotic women is worth dodging a few bullets. There is also the sense of duty and pride in a job well done.

He and his buddy rescue Marina and are blindsided by the striking, broken woman who mistakes them for Stronghold Tech. Before they can figure out how she knows about the elite securities team or find and eliminate their mark, the enemy discovers their hideout. Capture would be a fate worse than death and it looms so close Oliver and Marina can french it.

Betrayals meet harsh light and the fun-loving soldier is forced to face cruel reality. His damsel in distress is the one to blame, especially when Stronghold forces show, adding chaos to the kabooms. The dire situation turns deadly and Marina holds the key.

If only Oliver can stop loving and hating her long enough to get the answers.

Megan Mitcham was born and raised among the live oaks and shrimp boats of the Mississippi Gulf Coast, where her enormous family still calls home. She attended college at the University of Southern Mississippi where she received a bachelor's degree in curriculum, instruction, and special education. For several years Megan worked as a teacher in Mississippi. She married and moved to South Carolina and began working for an international non-profit organization as an instructor and co-director.

In 2009 Megan fell in love with books. Until then, books had been a source for research or the topic of tests. But one day she read *Mercy* by Julie Garwood. And oh, Mercy, she was hooked!

Megan lives in Southern Arkansas where she pens heart pounding romantic thriller novels and window-steaming erotic romance. For information on releases and giveaways subscribe at meganmitcham.com!

Facebook: AuthorMeganMitcham
Twitter: @MeganMMMitcham
Pinterest: MeganMitcham5
Goodreads: Megan_Mitcham
Website: www.meganmitcham.com

FOR INFORMATION ON NEW RELEASES &
GIVEAWAYS, SIGN UP FOR MEGAN'S
NEWSLETTER AT WWW.MEGANMITCHAM.COM.

www.ingramcontent.com/pod-product-compliance
Lightning Source LLC
Chambersburg PA
CBHW070752120626
46557CB00002B/563